D0348968

Praise

A HARD WITCHING

AND OTHER STORIES

"Baker shows in this debut collection an impressive precision and control. . . . A writer to watch." —*Quill & Quire*

"Masterful and thoroughly enjoyable. . . . A book to reread, twice as good the second time. Jacqueline Baker, with an honest and skillful debut, surpasses the crowd by miles."
—*The Globe and Mail*

"After spending time with the memorable characters in the eight superbly crafted stories in this collection, readers will be left with an admiration for their will to survive. They deal not only with the unforgiving geography and climate, but the heartaches that life inevitably brings." —*Edmonton Journal*

"It would be too easy to characterize Baker as a western Canadian writer; she evokes more than that. Baker is strongly reminiscent of Annie Proulx in her depictions of the wide-open west, and the places and spaces in the hearts of those there. . . . [*A Hard Witching*] is highly charged and tighter than taut."
—*The Hamilton Spectator*

"Jacqueline Baker is one of the most talented writers I have ever read. Imagine sipping a fine wine filled with character and flavour." —*The Lethbridge Herald*

"[Baker's] stories are steeped in a rich sense of rural familiarity. This book compares favourably to two other recent Prairie collections, Sharon Butala's *Real Life* and Gloria Sawai's *A Song for Nettie Johnson*." —*The Gazette* (Montreal)

"Prose like this proves both Baker's talent and potential."
—*Winnipeg Free Press*

Jacqueline Baker

A Hard Witching
and other stories

HarperPerennialCanada

A PHYLLIS BRUCE BOOK

A Hard Witching and Other Stories
© 2003 by Jacqueline Baker. All rights reserved.

A Phyllis Bruce Book, published by Harper-
*Perennial*Canada, an imprint of HarperCollins
Publishers Ltd

First published in hardcover by Phyllis Bruce
Books and Harper*Flamingo*Canada, imprints of
HarperCollins Publishers Ltd, 2003. This paper-
back edition 2004.

HarperCollins books may be purchased for
educational, business, or sales promotional use
through our Special Markets Department.

HarperCollins Publishers Ltd
2 Bloor Street East, 20th Floor
Toronto, Ontario, Canada
M4W 1A8

www.harpercanada.com

National Library of Canada Cataloguing in
Publication

Baker, Jacqueline
A hard witching and other stories / Jacqueline
Baker.

"A Phyllis Bruce book".
ISBN 0-00-639245-8

I. Title.

PS8553.A3793H37 2004   C813'.6
C2003-905662-7

RRD 9 8 7 6 5 4 3 2 1

Printed and bound in the United States
Set in Monotype Baskerville

for my mother,
and for Gabrielle & Julian

Cherry

I

He was our great-uncle (younger than my grandfather by a number of years, we were surprised to learn at the funeral), though Max and I always called him, simply, Uncle Aloetius. Because we spent long, dull summers with my grandparents, and because Uncle Aloetius was retired from his job at the pottery in Medicine Hat and now lived in the same small town near the hoodoo-like hills of the South Saskatchewan River valley, we saw quite a lot of him, though we never knew him well, never settled into the kind of teasing friendliness we enjoyed with my grandmother's brothers from distant Gravelbourg. And though Max and I never talked about it, I think we shared the same uneasiness about Uncle Aloetius, a result of more than just his disturbing habit of leaving the top two buttons of his trousers undone to accommodate the gout that had swelled his belly round and hard as a pumpkin— something Max and I might have found funny in someone else, someone other than Uncle Aloetius, with his tobacco voice and the fine purple veins cracking across his nose like lightning, and the way he would drop a meaty fist onto the table unexpectedly when talking, making the coffee cups jump and rattling us all in our chairs.

Despite his habit of blowing his nose loudly into a hanky at the supper table, despite his German accent (inexplicably heavier than our grandfather's), despite the tufts of hair on his knuckles and in his ears, Uncle Aloetius occupied a position outside our mockery of grown-ups, our low-grade jokes about smells and scabs and bodily functions. For this alone, this impossibility of caricature, we may have respected him, may even have liked him a little—wanted, in fact, to like him. And he, in turn, may have wanted us to. But there was something about Uncle Aloetius that defied both affection and ridicule. He would try to tease us, try to joke with us the way our grandfather did, easily, the way our other uncles did. But his humour always fell flat, as if he did not quite believe in it himself.

"Bet you a quarter you can't tear this leaf in half," he said one morning; not a jest, a demand. *Betchu a kvotteru cant dare dis leefenhuff.*

He held the poplar leaf out toward Max, who was sitting on one of the cinder blocks Grandma used to pot her geraniums. Max looked at me, then took the leaf in his palm carefully, as if it were a green heart, still beating. He fingered it briefly, squinted up at Uncle Aloetius and handed it to me.

"Right in half," Uncle Aloetius stressed. "Right down the middle there."

I used my thumbnails to edge minutely, painstakingly, down the spine, staying impeccably true to the line of it. Max breathed heavily, nostrils whistling, over my shoulder.

"Oh-oh," Uncle Aloetius said every few seconds, when it seemed I might falter.

I had to tilt the leaf away from the reflection of the sun to see the spine clearly. My elbows were propped on my knees to steady me; my hands kept from trembling through sheer force of will. When I was finished, I handed over the two perfect halves.

"That's good," Uncle Aloetius said, studying them carefully. "Pretty good." He held one half up. "That's a good half." Then, tearing that half in two, he added, "Here's a quarter."

When Uncle Aloetius didn't joke, when he talked to us seriously, as an adult would, there was something else, not quite cruelty, but something like it.

"Bet you can't guess what I got here," he said to us one afternoon, coming into my grandparents' yard with a small cardboard box under his arm.

It was Thanksgiving weekend, and though it was cold, Max and I sat on the gravel driveway, idly throwing stones onto the roof of the garage.

No, we confessed uneasily, we couldn't.

"Come on, now," he barked, "just guess."

Max looked at me as if he might cry. Uncle Aloetius had played this game with us before. Chances were, whatever was in the box was something alive, or something that had recently been alive or, worse still, only a part of something that had recently been alive: gopher tails (*ten cents apiece ven I vus your aitch, enuff to pie a new pair uff shews*); the grey, pointed head of a sturgeon he'd caught in the river; a rattle from the snake he'd run over on the highway.

"I don't know," I said slowly, trying not to imagine the terrible options. "Partridge feathers?"

"Partridge feathers," he scoffed, and shook his head. He settled the box on the gravel and pried the lid off with the tip of his walking stick. "Have a look."

Max remained stolidly near the garage, but I took a step or two forward, thinking, Please God, let it not be a snake, anything but a snake.

I peeked into the box. It wasn't a snake, it wasn't alive, and it hadn't been alive recently, not by any stretch of the imagination. I wrinkled my nose, leaned away slightly, hoping Uncle Aloetius wouldn't notice. Made confident by the fact that I had not shrieked or bolted, Max sidled over.

"Ew," he said simply.

Uncle Aloetius frowned at us, annoyed and disappointed. "A *skull*," he said, as if we didn't get it. "Look at those teeth there."

Reluctantly, we looked. They were blackened and broken and clamped in a vicious grin. I considered, briefly, the awful possibility of a tongue.

"Bobcat," he said proudly. *Popcat.* "Here." He held it out to us. Max and I stepped back. "It's petrified," he stressed, and tapped his knuckles against his forehead. "Like wood."

Petrified.

"Like a vossle," he added.

Max and I blinked.

"A *vossle*," he shouted. "Don't they teach you that?"

Max sniffled, grabbed the hem of my shirt. Of course, I knew he meant fossil, but I couldn't admit this, knowing it would make him even more scornful. In dealing with Uncle Aloetius, we'd learned, there was a measure of safety in ignorance. He was more willing to give up if he thought us merely stupid.

"What the Christ *do* they teach you?"

Max always cracked under the pressure.

"Pictures," he bawled, "with macaroni."

Uncle Aloetius, still holding the skull forward, scowled at the two of us, stared at my hands fixed firmly in my pockets, at the snot pooling above Max's quivering lip. Then he packed up the skull and hobbled off toward home, stabbing the air with his walking stick every few steps, as if still making his point.

Uncle Aloetius lived across town in a small grey stuccoed house flanked by several overgrown lilac bushes and filled with his collections, things he'd found while walking the Sand Hills or down by the river or in the fields blown smooth in spring. Pieces of things: skulls, bones and skins. They ranged across shelves and counters and window ledges, were nailed to walls, rested unexpectedly in kitchen drawers and closets and dressers. Not that Max or I ever ventured far during our visits to Uncle Aloetius' house, choosing to remain quietly perched on either side of our grandfather like bookends. But we were occasionally sent to fetch some small item—more mix from the back bedroom, the calendar from the kitchen cupboard, a deck of cards, or a knife, or a glass—a task that would most often end in an unhappy discovery of some sort.

It was always me, not Max, who made these discoveries. Being older, I didn't mind so much that I was the one appointed to run the errands. Foraging in dark bedrooms and closets would have been easier, though, if Max had come with me. At first I bullied him into it, staring fiercely at him until he slid from his seat and followed me from the room.

"Just reach in there and find the bottle opener," I said one time, pointing to the kitchen drawer, which we'd been able to wedge open only a few inches before it stuck.

"Why don't you?"

"Your hand's smaller." I lifted my hand, spreading the fingers wide. "See?"

Max stared.

"Hold up your hand, Max."

Max stuck both hands firmly down the front of his pants.

I knew not to force the issue. If he cried, things would go worse for us with Uncle Aloetius and with my grandfather, too, who suffered our squeamishness only in small and sporadic doses.

I slipped my hand into the drawer, shuddering as I felt around, recognizing objects by touch—scissors, a pen, rubber bands, nothing worse than that. When I found what I thought was the bottle opener, I slid my hand out quickly, relieved. But it wasn't a bottle opener. I had grabbed instead the handle of a small hairbrush, a soft blue enamel one rimmed with a border of white vines. A woman's brush. And I thought immediately of Uncle Aloetius' wife, Cherry, whom I knew only through photographs. At any other time, I would have been thrilled to find the brush, fascinated as I was by her, by her long absence and, because of it, her perpetual youth. But on that day I was too dismayed at the thought of having to slide my hand back into that drawer to pay much attention to a hairbrush. That day, it was merely another strange item in an already strange house.

When I finally found the opener, I puffed out a great sigh of relief.

Max pulled his hands from his pants and said, "See, they're not smaller."

"Next time," I said firmly, as we returned to the living room, "it's your turn."

From then on, Max gazed stubbornly back at me whenever I was called on to fetch something, and I ended up going miserably alone.

There was one place in Uncle Aloetius' house even I would not go, upon pain of death.

"You know what's down there?" Uncle Aloetius would say each visit without fail, nodding toward the door—latched shut with hooks at both the top and bottom—leading from his kitchen to the root cellar.

Max and I shook our heads, though of course we knew. How could we forget?

"Do you?" he'd demand.

"Children," Max would say, chin trembling. "Lots of them." What kind of children?"

"Bad ones."

"And were you good this week?"

God, yes, we hoped so.

Naturally, we had questions about these children—*How many? Where did they come from? How old were they?* and the one that gripped Max: *Where did they go to the bathroom?*—questions we broached in bed at night with the blankets pulled up over us like a tent and Max's feet pressed against my belly, or, more often, safely by daylight. But they were questions we would never ask Uncle Aloetius.

We did, after much deliberation, ask my grandmother one morning while she mended clothes in front of the TV.

"It's those Germans," she said, as if that explained everything. "Just look," she added, "at their fairy tales." She bit a thread between her broad front teeth, teeth we always thought looked like Chiclets. "Russian Germans," she said, meaning Grandpa and Uncle Aloetius, "they're the worst."

"Are we Germans?" Max asked after a moment. "Russian Germans?"

"Part," she said. "A quarter."

Max started to cry then. Grandma put down the work sock she was darning, pulled out the damp wad of Kleenex she always kept balled up in her sleeve (the *same* Kleenex? we often wondered) and wiped at Max's face.

"Oh, now," she said, "that's just foolish."

For a long time, though, we weren't sure whether she meant the possibility of children kept chained for years in Uncle Aloetius' cellar or simply Max's tears.

But Max was like that. There was always a certain element of desperation to his fear that made me sorry for him on those visits to Uncle Aloetius' house, sorrier than I was for myself. I could, for instance, almost feel the trembling of poor Max's limbs through the plaid chesterfield when Uncle Aloetius addressed either of us. Uncle Aloetius must have sensed it, too, smelled the fear coming off Max like the panic off a trapped rabbit. And he must have despised it.

"Max," he said unexpectedly one night, as he and my grand-father leaned over a card table playing rookie, "get my glasses from the bedroom."

It was quite late on an evening in December, and the house was dark except for the old teardrop floor lamp that stood in the corner behind Uncle Aloetius' chair and the faint, almost-pretty green glow of the neighbours' Christmas lights coming through the front room windows layered over heavily with ice. "The Little Drummer Boy," our favourite carol, played softly on the turntable, but sounded fuzzy because Uncle Aloetius needed to replace the needle. Every so often it would skip, and either Grandpa or Uncle Aloetius would thump his boot against the floor to fix it. The air was stuffy and old, and my skin itched hotly beneath my long underwear. Neither Max nor I had removed our parkas, and we held our toques and mittens between our knees hopefully, as though we would be leaving any second.

"Max," Uncle Aloetius repeated, "go get my glasses."

Max did not move. Though I couldn't see his face from where I was sitting on the other side of Grandpa, I knew how he would look, his lips stretched tight and pale with anxiety.

"I'll get them," I offered quickly.

"Max can do it," Grandpa said reasonably, taking a drink from the tumbler of warm rye and coke at his elbow. He shuffled neatly through the deck a couple of times with his thumbs and looked down at Max, who still had not moved.

"Max!" he said.

I clenched my jaw, knowing Max would cry, knowing his tears would bring all kinds of anger and derision down upon both our heads: the candy-assed kids from the city, the cryba-bies, the chickenshits.

"Get Uncle's glasses," Grandpa barked, elbowing Max in the shoulder. "What are you waiting for?"

I looked across the table at Uncle Aloetius, expecting that old scornful look of disdain. But he was staring at my grandfa-ther, looking at him with a raw kind of emotion, part resent-ment, part relief, his face open like a wound. And I thought, for the first time, with absolute amazement, They're *brothers.* I was so shocked to think of them that way, to make such a blood dis-covery, so embarrassed to see Uncle Aloetius naked, almost needful, that, without thinking, I grabbed at my grandfather's wrist.

"Let's go," I said. "Let's go home."

But no one heard me. On the turntable, the record had begun to skip at the chorus. Max stood, paused a moment, not looking at anybody, and then walked slowly down the dark hallway toward the bedroom, his snowsuit rasping with each step, the record continuing to skip and the three of us staring after him, as if we were momentarily suspended and preserved in that cold green winter light.

When Max returned, grim-faced, glasses in hand, Grandpa thumped his boot against the floor, and the music and the card playing resumed, steadily, as if nothing in that room had changed.

II

They were the only boys in a family of five, one of those typical Saskatchewan farm families, except that neither Grandpa
nor Uncle Aloetius ever had any interest in farming. So when
the time came, the land was divided among the three girls and
their husbands—who *did* want to farm, as the girls were quick
to point out—and the boys were left to make their own ways.
Grandpa got on almost immediately with the R.M. (meaning,
Grandma explained, "rural municipality," not "arm," as Max
and I had thought), doing road service, a good, steady job,
and Uncle Aloetius wandered around to Kindersley and Swift
Current and Lethbridge, finally getting work at the pottery in
Medicine Hat, where he settled. It wasn't clear exactly where
he'd met Aunt Cherry, but she was with him when he arrived
in Medicine Hat. They rented a tiny apartment across from
the old stockyards on Foundry Street and were married soon
after, at the family homestead in Saskatchewan. They did not
linger after the wedding, but returned to the city and their little apartment, which no doubt stank all day of manure and
slaughter.

They wouldn't have seen much of each other in those early
years, Grandpa and Uncle Aloetius. Holidays maybe, the occasional weekend, more often once Grandpa bought a car.
Everyone thought Uncle Aloetius had moved to Medicine Hat
for good. Even after Cherry left, no one expected him to come
home. And he didn't. I imagined him alone in that little two-
room apartment, smelling the hot dark smell of animal flesh
that got into his clothes and his hair and his skin, that left a
faint taste in the food he ate; imagined him listening all night to
the moaning of cattle penned shank to shank in the heat and
the rain and the snow, and beneath that another sound, lower,

the constant hum of flies. No one could figure out what made him stay, but stay he did.

So when he bought that little house just four blocks from Grandpa, turning up one day with his belongings packed roof-high into the back of his old white Pontiac, we were all surprised. "Why would I live there," he said in response, meaning Medicine Hat, "when I can live here at half the price and none of the headache?" For Uncle Aloetius had never made any bones about his distaste for the city, in spite of the fact that he'd lived there nearly forty years.

"Those people," he'd say in disgust, and swat his hand through the air.

By the time Aunt Cherry had left Uncle Aloetius to go back east to Ontario, Grandpa had met and married Grandma. They had three children, two who died in infancy and the third, my father. This was after the war, during that brief time of good rainfall and good wheat prices, and Grandpa and Grandma were busy managing their own lives, their little family. Grandpa built them a house across from the lumberyard— a small two-storey frame house—and planted an enormous garden out back from which Grandma put up pickles and preserves each fall. From what my grandmother told me in later years, it sounded like a good life, though her memory might have been taking the edge off things, as memory does.

A few years after Grandpa died, she told me she'd known him almost a year before she was aware he had a brother.

"Your grandpa had come down to see me once," she said, "just after he bought that car, that awful old thing, and he said, 'Ludie, I think I'll take a ride over to Medicine Hat next week, if you want to come.' We were engaged by then, of course, so I said, 'I don't mind if I do,' and he said, 'I guess there'll be room for both of us with Aloise,' and I said, 'Aloise? Who's Aloise?' and he just looked around a bit and then he said, 'My brother.'"

III

Grandpa had never shared Uncle Aloetius' penchant for collecting, but he occasionally joined him on his meandering walks through the Sand Hills north of town or in the deep, stratified coulees of the river hills. If Max and I happened to be visiting, we were expected to participate. Though we hated those long, hot, agonizingly boring walks, whether through the Sand Hills or the river hills, we always chose the Sand Hills if consulted. For one reason, there were no rattlers, curled like fat grey muscles behind rocks and beneath ground cedar, and no bull snakes either, which, though harmless (as Grandpa continually pointed out), could startle us both into tears by appearing suddenly in the sagebrush at our feet, long and black and thick as a man's arm. For another, the Sand Hills were full of chokecherries and saskatoons, and we could sit on the great flesh-coloured dunes, writing our names with sticks and letting the hot, soft sand squish up between our toes, pretending to be marooned on a desert island, pretending the dry, rolling scrubland for miles around us was all water. We could pick bunches of wild rose, which smelled faintly of apples, and scurf-pea and orange sand dock to take home to our grandmother, and if we were lucky, we might see a bush hare or a buck or even a mule deer and her fawn feeding in the small shade of aspen bluffs. Usually, though, we were not allowed to wander off by ourselves or sit alone under that vast blue sky, but were expected to keep pace with my grandfather and Uncle Aloetius, who, much to our dismay, did not walk on the dunes at all. They preferred to poke through the brush, where we were subjected to the awful zinging of grasshoppers against our bare legs and arms and faces and where, as Uncle Aloetius claimed, we were more likely to find some good thing: antelope prongs bleached white by the sun or petrified snail shells or even a Clovis point.

"What's a Clovis point, anyway?" Max asked me one day— in that last summer before Uncle Aloetius died—as we minced along behind him, eyes glued to the ground, ever wary of a chance rattler that may have found its way up from the river hills, or of other terrible discoveries: a dead kangaroo rat or a salamander or simply cow shit.

"An arrowhead," I said, "I think."

Grandpa was off to the side a few feet, but Uncle Aloetius looked at us over his shoulder.

"About yay big." He held up his thumb. "Shaped," he said, "like your tongue."

Max felt his tongue.

"But chipped around the base, like so. For hunting." He raised his arms in an absurd gesture meant, we assumed, to denote great size. "*Voolly mammet.*"

"Really?" Max said. "Woolly mammoths?"

"Yah." Uncle Aloetius nodded. "Ten thousand years old. More." He stopped walking and turned to stare out across the field. "They used to be all over here." He swung his walking stick through the air. "Before that," he said, "it was all ice. There was nothing."

Max looked at him in disbelief. "Where did it go, all the ice?"

Uncle Aloetius shrugged. "Melted. Dried up. Ran away. Now there's just the river."

"And buffalo?" Max asked. "Was there buffalo?"

"That was later." Uncle Aloetius scowled, though you could

see he was pleased. "Thousands of years. Prehistoric times. There's rubbing stones still. In the glacial tillage." He stopped and frowned down at us. "You know what that is?"

"Yeah," Max said, "sure."

I glared at him.

"And teepee rings," Uncle Aloetius said, walking again. "It took seven, eight buffalo hides to make a teepee. Cartilage to sew it together. Bones and hooves to make glue. The stomach for a water pouch. Or a cooking pot. They wasted nothing," he added proudly, as if it had all been under his personal supervision.

"What did they use the heart for?" Max asked.

"They ate it," he said, "of course. Same as *kow harst*."

I grimaced at Max, ready to band in solidarity against the detested cow heart Grandma sometimes sliced, breaded and fried at Grandpa's or Uncle Aloetius' request. But he had trotted ahead to walk abreast of Uncle Aloetius. Grandpa stopped a few feet away.

"It was a special treat, buffalo heart," Uncle Aloetius said, "for an honoured brave. Or some favoured member of the tribe."

"They ate it?" Max asked.

"Didn't I just say so?"

"Raw," Max asked, "or cooked?"

Grandpa walked over, took the canteen Uncle Aloetius carried slung across his shoulder. "When we were young," he interrupted, taking a big swig of water, "we used to come out here for fun, eh, Aloise?" He pointed to the highest of the dunes, which rose maybe fifteen metres or so above us. "We'd bring boards," he said, "and slide down."

"In the winter?" I asked.

"Summer, too," he said. "Or we'd just roll down. We'd roll the girls down. Like barrels. Remember that? They would scream."

Uncle Aloetius nodded.

"They would tie their skirts like so between their knees and we would roll them down and they would scream. They'd come up with sand in their hair and in their mouths. And laugh. Then we'd have a fire, maybe. Aloise," he said, "remember? Remember Eleanor Gutbergen? Huh?"

Uncle Aloetius shrugged.

Grandpa tipped his head toward Uncle Aloetius. "He remembers. All those girls, Eleanor Gutbergen. They all chased him. He was always the favourite."

Uncle Aloetius said nothing, just kept jabbing that stick around, turning over rocks, lifting branches of sage and ground cedar.

"We had fun times out here, eh, Aloise?"

"Did you ever find a Clovis point?" Max asked.

"Go." Grandpa nodded toward the dune. "Roll down. It's fun."

Max and I looked at each other.

"Go on," he said, smiling, though his voice sounded angry for some reason. "Try it."

Max and I walked slowly toward the dune, the sun beating down heavily on our heads. I touched the top of my hair. It was hot.

"Go on," Grandpa said.

Max started up the hill, leaning forward, using his hands against the incline for balance, his feet sinking to the ankles in sand. I looked down at my short skirt. It would be impossible to tie it between my knees, and I became furious suddenly that I had not worn shorts. I glanced back to see whether Grandpa would force me to go, but he was shading his eyes, peering up at Max, silhouetted now by the sun. Uncle Aloetius stood next to him, looking up also. And it occurred to me that neither of them would care whether I went up or not.

"Okay," Grandpa said when Max was poised at the top of the dune. "Just lay down and roll. Keep your arms straight at your sides."

For a moment, I thought Max would do it—it seemed as though he would. But then he just stood there, shifting his weight from one foot to the other.

"Oh, for Christ's sake," Grandpa called up, "it won't kill you. It's sand. The girls used to do it."

Max scratched the back of his arm.

"Did Grandma ever do it?"

"Grandma?" Grandpa said. "How the hell should I know? Probably."

Max stared down at us.

"Did Aunt Cherry?"

I started at the sound of that rarely heard name, surprised that Max would say it. Grandpa opened his mouth, snapped it shut. Uncle Aloetius kept looking up at Max as if he hadn't heard, or hadn't cared. Max stood at the top of the dune, waiting.

"Oh, for Christ's sake," Grandpa said again, but more quietly now. "Walk down, then."

Max hesitated, then scrambled down the hill, sliding most of the way, the sand rushing before him in a smooth, hot sheet. When he reached the bottom, I whispered, "Why'd you say that? Why'd you bring up Aunt Cherry?" But he just walked over to Uncle Aloetius and asked, "What colour was it? The Clovis point?"

Grandpa frowned. "We should get back, not?"

"Yah." Uncle Aloetius shrugged. "If you want to get back."

"No, Grandpa," Max said, "let's look for a Clovis point. We can find one, I bet."

Grandpa shook his head. "We should get back," he said, and

without waiting for the rest of us started walking to where the car sat white and shimmering in the heat, like a bone.

IV

Of Aunt Cherry, Max and I knew little. We had glimpsed a photograph of her in Uncle Aloetius' bedroom, but for obvious reasons had never lingered over it. There were two others in my grandmother's album. The first was a rather distant shot of a bride and groom standing solemnly on the steps of the Catholic church in town. They were both frowning a little, perhaps at the sun, and held their arms straight at their sides, Cherry's plastic bouquet half covered by the white dress that flared out a little at her knees. The only indication they were even aware of each other's presence was their shoulders pressed firmly together. Underneath, my grandmother had written in neat blue pencil, *Cherry and Aloetius*.

Next to that photograph was another of the two of them, but this time with my grandfather, almost unrecognizable in a clean white shirt and suspenders, a fedora cocked to one side over his unhandsome face. He lounged easily between them, an arm slung across each of their shoulders, his mouth partway open. Uncle Aloetius stood almost as solemn as before—as though bearing all my grandfather's weight in that arm— except that something in his face had relaxed. Not a smile, not quite, but the closest thing to it I'd ever seen on Uncle Aloetius. On this younger man, this boy, thin and pale in his dark suit, that smile made any relation to the man we knew—the man of the gout and the suspenders and the walking stick—all but inconceivable. Yet something in the young man's expression was unaccountably Uncle Aloetius, some element of anxiety, as if nothing light came easily to him. In that photograph, he reminded me sometimes of Max, though I couldn't have said why, and I didn't like the parallel. Some tension in the line of the jaw, perhaps, nothing more. Serious, even on his wedding day. It made me wonder, had he never been happy?

Cherry was something else entirely. In the second photograph, she had turned halfway around, her teeth bared in what looked to be a laugh, as though Grandpa had just said something tremendously funny. The hand that held the bouquet had blurred now, being raised or lowered, we couldn't tell. Three other people were in the photograph, anonymous people, two men, and a woman in a frumpy knee-length dress and a hat with a veil. But they stood rigidly, staring straight ahead. At first, we'd thought the woman was Grandma, but she'd said, "No, I didn't know your grandpa then. That was before my time."

A dog had wandered into the frame, too, his head and front leg just visible in the foreground, tongue lolling in a crazy grin. Max said it must have been Grandpa's dog; he could tell by how the dog was looking right at Grandpa. But I didn't see how Max could tell that. The dog could have been looking at any one of them, at no one. The top corner of the snapshot had been torn away, just a chunk of sky, the edge of a cottonwood tree, that was all. Beneath this photograph my grandmother had written simply, *With Mattias*.

V

The morning we heard Uncle Aloetius was dead, Max and I were out in the garden picking what would certainly be the last of the peas, the plants still cool and swollen with the night air, and Uncle Aloetius—as far as we knew—still across town smoking happily, or at least not unhappily, in the old leatherette recliner on his front porch, cap tipped far back on his head the way he always wore it and a thermos of Nescafé between his knees. It was late August, and the sun had already bleached the edges of leaves and baked the earth too solid for a hoe. Grandpa came over from the neighbours', hauling their Rototiller, ready to till up the pea plants when we had finished. He scooped a handful of pods from the metal bucket and unzipped one, dragging the peas out in one smooth motion with his thumb.

"Eat some," he said. "They put hair on your chest."

The phone rang in the kitchen, and Grandpa asked us if we knew how to make a peapod into a whistle, and Grandma came to the back door and stood barefoot on the edge of the steps, frowning at us as if she had forgotten something, and Grandpa dropped the empty pods and walked over, but only halfway, and they just looked at each other, their hands hanging motionless at their sides, with the morning's first cabbage butterflies like tissue paper everywhere and the cool green smell of peapods.

And then Grandma said, "Aloetius."

Grandpa stood there a bit longer.

"What is it?" Max said.

"Come." Grandma waved us in through the screen door. We went to stand by the window, and Grandma came up behind us, said, "Leave him alone now." But she watched too, a hand on each of our shoulders, as Grandpa fired up the Rototiller and began plowing through the garden, not just through the peas but through unharvested pumpkin and squash and rows of corn. Max and I looked at each other and then at our grandmother, her mouth settled into its usual puzzling calm.

"Grandma," Max said, "what's wrong?"

But she just sighed and lifted her shoulders a little.

"Someone should go out there, I guess," she said, finally. "Before he does something foolish."

VI

"I guess you'll call Cherry," my grandmother said that evening at supper, after phone calls had been placed to relatives and arrangements made for Uncle Aloetius' funeral. She said it evenly, as if it were a fact, but from the way she looked at Grandpa, Max and I could tell it was a question. "She'll want to come back," she added.

We were eating much later than was typical with our grand-parents, the sun already at that point of descent when its power seemed unbearable. It was hot in the kitchen. On any other day, we might have filled our plates and sat in the shade on the back steps, listening to the after-supper sounds of lawn mowers and children and dishes clinking against each other through the open windows of our neighbours' kitchens. But this day we stayed at the table, as if in some sort of penance, our legs stick-ing to the vinyl of our chairs.

Grandpa mashed at his boiled potatoes, shook salt liberally over everything and began to eat without looking up. Grandma wiped her brow with a tea towel and took her seat. She picked up her fork, put it down, picked it up again. Max and I exchanged a glance across the table.

"Still in Thunder Bay." Grandma took a bite and chewed in that slow, careful way of hers, as though everything were rid-dled with fish bones. "From what I hear."

Thunder Bay. I loved the exotic, stormy sound of it, mouthed it quietly to myself, feeling the weight of it on my tongue. I imagined waves spraying a black shore, great pointed pines, wolves. I imagined lightning, brush fires sparked, then smothered, by the wild unpredictability of weather. I imagined smoke. Cherry; yes, if your name was Cherry, you would live in Thunder Bay. You would stand on the rocks, watching the storm roll in, rain whipping at your hair. You would have strong, beautiful hands. You would not, you could not, be married to a man like Uncle Aloetius.

Grandpa looked up, scowling into the sun that pounded through the kitchen window. "Pull that damn blind," he said to me.

I laid my fork carefully by my plate and got up, lifting my chair rather than scraping it against the linoleum as I usually did. Outside, a flock of noisy sparrows had gathered, shrieking and flapping over what remained of the garden. The tilled plants had already lost their greenness, lay wilted and browning in the heat, ears of corn rotting in their sleeves. There will be rats, I thought with a shiver, we'll get rats now.

No one had mentioned the garden since that morning, not since Grandma had said, "Someone should go out there, I guess." Max and I had watched from the window while Grandma, barefoot still, stepped steadily across the green swaths and pulled the key on the Rototiller. When the engine coughed itself out, Grandpa turned on her. *"Job foya mutt,"* he snarled. *Damn you to mud.*

But Grandma just stood there, and so he muttered, *"Es nutzt dich nicht,"* knowing she would not understand, using that ugly awful language against her, as he did when he was angry sometimes, against all of us. But it was nothing this time. *Mind your own business.* That was all. And Grandma said something back—we could see her lips move—but neither Max nor I could hear her. Maybe Grandpa couldn't either because he kept staring at her until she turned around, the key to the Rototiller wrapped in her palm. She walked back to the house, lifting one soiled foot and then the other across the swaths,

bending only once to collect the metal bucket of peas that Max
and I had left behind in the sun, as if that was her only reason
for going out there in the first place.

The key (though, oddly, not the Rototiller) had been
returned to the neighbours', and the bucket stood now in the
cool of the back porch, the peas waiting to be shelled,
blanched, packed in clear plastic bags labelled neatly with the
date on a strip of masking tape and frozen. They would be, I
knew. Work was not left undone at my grandparents', not for
anything. Nothing was wasted. And I wondered, when they ate
those peas next winter, when Grandma pulled the bag from
the freezer, would she see that date and think of this day, this
one long day?

"Sit down," she said now behind me. "Finish eating." I
returned quietly to the table.

"I have Cherry's number," she said to Grandpa, "unless
she's moved." She paused, watching as Grandpa raised his
coffee mug. "But I don't think so. She would be there still, I
think."

Max wriggled in his chair and I tried to send him a warning
look—*don't speak, don't even move*—but he fiddled with his fork,
tapping it to some unidentifiable tune against the rim of his
water glass, *ting ting ting*.

"You can call after supper," Grandma said.

Ting ting ting ting.

"Or I could—"

"What for?" Grandpa finally spat, flecks of potato flying
from his lips. Max dropped his fork on the floor with a clatter
and we all stared at it. Grandpa wiped at his mouth with the
back of one hand. "So she knows the cheques won't come?"

"Mattias," my grandmother said.

"Thirty years she takes money from a man not even—"

"*Mattias.*" Grandma looked over at Max and me. Our

grandfather glanced at us briefly, pushed his plate away. Not even what? Not even thanking him? Not even visiting?

"She's his wife still," she said. "She should know."

"His wife," Grandpa sneered.

"It's been so long," Grandma said, leaning forward, "to keep blaming. Matt. Listen. After all this time. Who is there to blame?"

"Blame," he growled, head down. "You don't know."

I snuck a look at his face then, was shocked to see his nose was running, like a child's, the way Max's did, that he didn't bother to wipe it.

Outside, beyond the drawn blind, the sparrows lifted in a sudden rush, the way they do. The quick, rising sound of air being beaten, as if they were flying right at you, and then that impossible hot silence. Grandpa shook his head heavily.

"You don't know," he said again, but the force was gone now. It was an apology, of course. Somehow, we all knew it.

"Yes," Grandma said gently after a moment. She bent to pick up Max's fork, wiped it with the hem of her apron. "Yes, Matt. I do."

And whatever they were angry about seemed to be over then. But later I thought about what they had said. That Aunt Cherry took money from Uncle Aloetius, a man not even— what? Not even her husband? But, no, she was his wife still, Grandma had said. There were the photographs from the wedding; I'd seen them. So, what?

I asked Max about it that night, long after we'd climbed into bed, after the door to Grandpa and Grandma's bedroom softly closed, after the long summer light yellowing the walls had finally gone.

It took him so long to answer that I assumed he was already asleep, so I closed my eyes, too, felt the length of that day settle along my bones, until I heard him say, "Who cares."

But it was so late then, I couldn't be sure he'd spoken at all. The room was dark. I could have dreamed the words. And I thought, After all this time.

I had written her name out sometimes in the back of my school notebook, in big looping writing, with flourishes on the *A* and the *C* and the *M*. Aunt Cherry. Cherry. Cherry Mueller (though this last only rarely, as it called too vividly to mind images of Uncle Aloetius). We, Max and I, didn't blame her for leaving Uncle Aloetius. Who wouldn't? I imagined her fleeing across the prairies—her white wedding dress fluttering behind—to far-off, mythical Thunder Bay. Often, she became the heroine of our make-believe games, the princess fleeing the ogre.

Sensing the slightly illicit nature of these games, we would choose remote spots in which to indulge ourselves: the alley behind the house, the abandoned lot beside the post office; the garage. The last time we played was in the spare room upstairs, the day after Uncle Aloetius died. It was hotter up there, even with the windows open, so we stripped down to our underwear, though Max, for some reason, retained his socks.

"Max," I said, losing patience, "you can't be Aunt Cherry."

We went through this argument nearly every time, but on this day we had something new to fight over: an old wide-brimmed hat, mauve with a veil and yellow roses and a wide satin ribbon along the crown. It must have belonged to Aunt Cherry, we knew. It couldn't possibly have been our grand-mother's. Max clutched it against his bare chest.

"Max," I said, pulling at the hat, "let go. You're a boy. This is a girl's hat. See? Do you want to look like a girl?"

Max tugged, his face set in that bullish look.

"Okay," I said, letting go and crossing my arms, "go ahead. Make a fool of yourself."

Max jammed the hat down on his head and pranced around on the tips of his toes, lifting his knees high, his long legs absurdly white. "I'm Aunt Cherry," he said in a ridiculous falsetto. "Look at me."

"Max," I said, snatching the hat away, "don't be stupid." I took these play-actings seriously, and for the first time I realized that to Max they were only games, nothing more. I realized that, to him, Aunt Cherry was no one, a photograph in an album. She might as well have been on the moon.

"Who can I be, then?" he said.

"You can be . . ." I considered, not without an element of animosity. "You can be Uncle Aloetius."

Max stared at me, appalled. "He's *dead*."

"Well, who do you want to be?" I snapped. "You can't be Aunt Cherry."

"What's going on up here?"

Our grandmother had appeared in the doorway silently, as she often did.

I touched the brim of the hat guiltily, was about to say, "Nothing," when Max piped up, "She wants to be Aunt Cherry. She wishes she was her." And then he added, though I'd never said this, "She wishes Aunt Cherry was our grandma." And he laughed, pleased with his joke.

"Shut up, Max," I said.

He scowled at me. "You shut up."

Grandma looked slowly from one of us to the other, and I noticed she was wearing lipstick and her good dress—dark blue chiffon with a tiny white stripe and a full, swishing skirt—though we weren't expecting any relatives until the next day.

I wanted to say, "You look nice." She did, but at that moment I could not have said anything of the kind. There was something in her face very close to hurt. Or I thought there was, though maybe I just imagined it was there. Hurt was so unlike her. And for a second, for the first time in our lives, I hated Max, hated him so much that sweat broke out all over my body.

I thought Grandma might be angry, that she might punish us both. It was possible; so much that was strange had happened in the past few days.

But she just turned to leave, her skirt swirling out behind her. "Don't wreck that hat," was all she said, though at the stairs she added, "And for God's sake, don't let your grandfather hear you."

VII

Though Grandma had offered to pick her up at the airport in Medicine Hat, Aunt Cherry insisted on renting a car and driving herself the hundred or so miles. This seemed perfectly right to me, that she would return to Uncle Aloetius the same way she had left (or, at least, the same way I'd imagined she had left): on her own.

When Grandma told him, Grandpa simply snorted and flipped a page of the newspaper he was reading. We were sitting in the living room waiting for Aunt Cherry to arrive. On the coffee table stood a glass bowl of late summer flowers— larkspur and calendula and marigold—that I had picked that afternoon in honour of Aunt Cherry's arrival.

We all sat there, Max and I grudgingly at either end of the chesterfield (we had not spoken since the fight of the previous day), Grandpa and Grandma in their chairs by the window.

"Why don't you two go pick saskatoons out back," Grandma said finally. "We'll have them with some ice cream. When Aunt Cherry gets here."

"Saskatoons?" I said doubtfully, considering their sweet dirt taste, their gravelly bodies, the colour of a bruise. They weren't much of an offering. "Don't they have saskatoons," I asked, "in Thunder Bay?"

"So," she said, "pick them anyway. It's a nice thought." She went to the kitchen and rinsed out an old ice cream pail she'd been using for vegetable peelings. Max and I stood behind her, waiting for the pail, and I realized that a significant portion of the time we spent at our grandparents' was devoted to picking things: tomatoes and rhubarb and lettuce from the garden (the carrots, radishes and beets were all off-limits, as Max broke the stems, leaving the vegetables to rot in the earth); saskatoons and chokecherries out at the Sand Hills for jelly; mint and chamomile from the patch in back for the detested tea, which, along with raw garlic and nutmeg, was used to treat all the minor ailments that we didn't have the good sense to hide.

It had attained ritual proportions for us, this harvesting, our methods guided by our grandfather's counsel: always work left to right, so you don't miss anything; never pull, always pinch; pick with your right, hold (the bucket, the branch, the plant) with your left. Most important, pick early in the day, before the heat has sucked out all the night dew. We generally remained faithful to these rules, even if Grandpa wasn't around. Often we ate as we worked (there was no rule against this) and made up little songs that we thought terribly funny, punning tunes we'd heard on the radio: *Pardon me, boooy, is that the cat that chewed your new shoooes?* to "Chattanooga Choo-Choo" or *Don't ever leee-eave your pi-zza burning* to "Beast of Burden" (though Max always wanted to sing to "Convoy," which was impossible).

But this morning we did not sing. We trailed out to the saskatoon bushes west of the garage, me walking ahead with the ice cream pail, Max scuffing a few feet behind. We did not sing, nor did we eat as we picked. We kept our backs to each other, the pail on the ground between us. In the past few days, Max had seemed somehow different, less silly and less anxious, older perhaps. But there was something else, a sort of reserved hostility I'd never noticed about him before. Timed as it was, this change seemed to be connected to Uncle Aloetius' death, though I didn't see how that was possible. Uncle Aloetius hadn't really meant much to either of us. He was just an old man. Worse, he was Uncle Aloetius. And he was dead. That Max might be grieving seemed absurd to me, and I wondered if this change was just a show, a way of getting attention. I worried, too, about what he would say to Aunt Cherry. Would he tell her about our play-acting, about *my* play-acting? Would he make some stupid, hurtful joke as he'd done the previous day with Grandma?

I cut a look at him from the corner of my eye. He was picking slowly, dropping each berry into the pail before reaching for another.

"You shouldn't have said that to Grandma," I began after a moment. "That was a dumb thing to say."

I kept picking, waiting for him to respond. When he didn't, I turned around. He was crouched down, with his back to me.

"Max," I said, "I'm talking to you."

But he just shifted slightly on his haunches. I wanted desperately to know what he was staring at, but I turned back to my picking anyway. For a while, there was only the *plunk* and roll of my berries hitting the bottom of the ice cream pail. Finally, I turned to him. We were both dressed in our next-to-best clothes, had been warned against staining them or snagging them on the branches. For a second, I thought of shoving him, right between his narrow shoulder blades, into the bushes. I wished him there, caught in those branches, scraped and struggling. Instead, in spite of myself, I walked up to him and peeked over his shoulder. In the palm of his hand he held one fat saskatoon berry.

"What," I said, trying to sound uninterested, "are you looking at?"

"Watch," he said, and rolled the berry slightly with the tip of one finger in a way that made me think of the Mexican jumping beans our parents sometimes bought us at Woolworth's.

"So?" I was about to say, when a tiny worm, fine as an eyelash and white-white against that purple flesh, twisted up out of the berry and made an absurd, desperate movement, as though rearing its head like a rattler: a movement of aggression or blindness, it could have been either. And it was, for some reason, the most awful, the most terrible thing I had ever seen. I hit Max's hand hard harder than I'd meant to. The blow threw him off balance and he toppled onto his side in the dust, the berry landing with a leafy *thunk* in the bushes.

He looked simply startled at first, then his face grew tight and red. "What'd you do that for?" he yelled.

I was sorry I'd done it, and did not know why I had. I didn't know what to say, so I went back to picking, leaving him sprawled on the ground, my body tensed, half expecting him to charge me from behind, pummeling me into the bushes. He didn't, though, so I picked on, trying to act as if nothing had happened, even though I felt angry and ashamed and frightened, not of Max or of anything he could do to me, not of anything physical, not even of anything he could say to Grandma or Grandpa or Aunt Cherry in retaliation. I was afraid of something in me, something in both of us. I turned around and looked down at him, his mouth working silently, as though he were searching for words, terrible words, German words maybe; I looked down at that angry little face, the tender white rim over his ears and neck where he'd just gotten a haircut, and I loved him fiercely, so much it made my skin burn, loved him for holding that ugliness in his palm, that ugliness that had made me think, There is nothing good anymore. And I knew I would cry then. I pretended to pick some more, and as I did I felt something subside, felt something sink a little, because I knew somehow this was the last summer for us, the last summer we would come to this place. Uncle Aloetius was dead and he'd taken something with him, something terrifying and tender and unnameable.

When I finally looked back, Max was gone.

VIII

It took me a while to pick enough berries to make a bowlful. I knew Max wouldn't return to help; he was a sulker, we both were. When I finally walked back around the garage, a car I didn't recognize was parked behind Grandpa's Buick under the old cottonwood tree, and I thought, with a great flutter of my stomach, Aunt Cherry.

But when I stepped into the kitchen with the bucket clenched tightly in my hand, it was not Aunt Cherry sitting at the table with Grandma. I was both relieved and disappointed. Grandma and the other woman turned to me as I stood in the doorway, made awkward by the presence of this stranger. Neither Max nor Grandpa was in the room.

"Dump those in the sink," Grandma said, "with some cold water to soak."

I crossed the kitchen stiffly, noticing that the woman watched me with a funny sort of half-smile as I went. She was old, much older than Grandma, though it was hard to tell that at first because her hair was an odd flat shade of red and her eyelids were smeared heavily with green shadow that glittered, but softly, like new snow. She leaned with both elbows on the kitchen table, arms folded. In one hand she held a cigarette, and on her finger she wore a big gold ring in the shape of a cat's head, with two little green stones for eyes. It was hideous, but I couldn't look away. The woman caught my stare.

"You like this?" she said, wriggling her finger. "It's a present. From a sweetheart of mine."

The word *sweetheart* sounded so strange on her lips, a foreign word, and at first I didn't understand it, as though I'd never heard it before.

She took a long drag on her cigarette. "You got a sweetheart?" she said, letting the smoke puff out with each word. "I bet she's got a couple." But she wasn't even looking at me. I felt the back of my neck grow hot, slowly, the way it did when the sun hit it dead on. Grandma smiled at me a little, and I noticed she was wearing lipstick again, and I thought, It makes her mouth appear so odd, like when you cut different features from a magazine and put them all together for a new face. Her lips didn't quite seem to belong.

"Can't you say hello?" Grandma said to me.

"That's all right," the woman said, "she don't know me. I'm your Great-Auntie Geraldine." She said the last part loudly. If Max had been there, we would have snickered. And I remembered then about Max and I felt angry with this woman at the table, with her minty-smelling cigarette and her ugly gold ring, as if what had happened between Max and me had something to do with her.

"I'm your Great-Auntie Geraldine," she said again. "From Thunder Bay. That's in Ontario."

I stared at her a moment, then at my grandmother, then back again, with that awful feeling in my stomach of cold, slow dawning.

"She's been waiting for you all day," Grandma said to the woman. "They both have." Then she looked around the kitchen, noticing Max's absence. "Where's Max?" she asked.

But I just stood there, feeling sick. "Geraldine . . . ?" I said finally.

"*Auntie* Geraldine," the woman stressed.

"The kids know you as Cherry," Grandma explained.

"Oh," the woman said laughing, though not kindly, "that's right." She smirked at me. "Cherry," she said, "is how they used to say Gerri."

"They?" I said, though I didn't really want to know.

"Your grandpa," she said, "Aloetius. All those Germans. Isn't that right, Ludie?"

Grandma glanced at me, but said nothing.

"Can't say their *g*'s right," she went on, "or their *j*'s. Or their *th*'s or their *sh*'s. Or anything, really. Cherry." She made that same laughing sound again. "Cheraldine." She shook her head, as if she couldn't believe it. "'Tree o'clock,' they would say, 'Cheraldine, it's chust about tree o'clock.'" She shook her head again, looked from me to my grandma and back again, waiting for us to laugh, too.

"More coffee?" Grandma asked instead.

"Now you're talking," the woman said. "But I need to use the ladies' room first. I'm about to float away."

I watched her walk down the hall, watched the heavy brush of her old-woman thighs in the stretchy green fabric of her pants, the way her skin hung loosely at the backs of her elbows, like pouches.

"Where's Max?" Grandma asked behind me.

• • •

I went to bed that night without Max for the first time in all the summers we'd spent at our grandparents'. He had come back around suppertime with Grandpa, and though I'd tried to catch his eye across the table while we ate, he kept his head down, did not even look at Aunt Gerri except to say a brief hello, and then got up and left with Grandpa again after they'd finished eating, leaving me and Grandma and Aunt Gerri to do the dishes and then sit uneasily at the kitchen table with an untouched plate of date squares between us, waiting for a reasonable hour at which we could say good night.

Grandma came to tuck me in, something she didn't normally do.

"I wonder what those two got themselves into," she said, meaning Max and Grandpa.

I lay there, staring up through the window at the sky's, halflight.

"I don't know," I said, but I knew where they were, we both did. And I did not feel angry about it or resentful, only a little sad.

"Well," she said, "somebody's got to do it. There's so much stuff in there, it will take a good while." She stood and pulled the blind down, so I had nowhere to look now except inside the room. "Still," she said, more to herself, "I thought he might have waited until after the funeral. He might have waited that long."

She pulled the blanket up under my arms and tucked it in tight. I could hear Aunt Gerri humming in the bathroom, where I knew she was standing in front of the tiny mirror, smoking and putting rollers in her flat red hair. We both listened a moment. It was a Christmas carol, "Good King Wenceslas."

Grandma studied my face, then patted my foot beneath the

covers. "It won't be the first time," she said, and I thought even then that I knew what she was talking about. "Anyway," she said, "it will be a long day tomorrow. Get some rest."

"You're not German," I said, as she moved toward the door.

"No," she said, laughing. "You know that."

She stood there at the end of the bed, and I noticed she'd wiped her lipstick off, or hadn't bothered to reapply it, and this was somehow comforting. I tried to picture Grandpa and Max across town, but I couldn't see them in that house, not without Uncle Aloetius, not with the hot earth sucking the light so fast from the sky. And I knew Grandma would not stay long with me; she did not like to linger over things. So I said softly, hoping it would not carry, "But you call her Cherry, not Gerri."

And she looked so strange then, sad maybe, or just thinking back, as if that name had meant something to her once, too.

"Oh," she sighed, "you just pick things up." She shrugged. "After a while, it all becomes the same."

I found Max asleep on the chesterfield the next morning, half covered over with the plaid blanket from the spare room upstairs. He had not changed into pyjamas but wore his T-shirt and shorts from the day before. Someone had placed kitchen chairs facing the length of the chesterfield so he would not roll off in his sleep.

My grandmother was already in the kitchen frying eggs and potatoes, and I could see my grandfather beyond her through the window, puttering around the open garage doors.

"Watch these potatoes," Grandma said. "I need to go down cellar."

I stood at the stove, turning the smoking potatoes with a spatula, and Grandpa came to the door.

"I need a hand," he said.

But before I could answer, Max came into the kitchen.

"Never mind," Grandpa said to me. "Max, come help clean up the car."

I stood at the window watching them swipe across the Buick with wet rags from the rain barrel, knowing how cold their hands would be from that water, which had not yet been warmed by the sun, and when Grandma came up she said, "Go on out there. Tell them breakfast is nearly ready."

I slipped into my shoes and was about to open the screen door when I saw Aunt Gerri sitting on the concrete steps, and I stopped without thinking, made an awkward motion to go back inside. She'd seen me hesitate, but pretended she hadn't noticed, looking the other way, out into the yard at Max and Grandpa. And I felt so bad that I had to go out.

"Morning," she said, when I sat down. She was smoking, a pack of cigarettes with a lighter tucked inside balanced on her knee. Her hair was still in rollers, and I noticed how thin it was, her pinkish scalp exposed between the rows. She was wearing eyeshadow again, but this time a light shade of mauve that did not glitter and made her skin look vaguely yellow.

She caught me staring. "I never smoked a day in my life," she said, "till I married Aloise."

"Oh," I said.

"That's how it is," she said. "That's how things are."

I felt she expected some sort of response, so I said, "We're from Saskatoon. Max and me."

"You got a sweetheart?" she asked, and I felt that old hotness on the back of my neck.

"No," I said.

She nodded, as if I'd said yes.

"How's Thunder Bay?" I asked, trying to make conversation.

"It's Thunder Bay," she said. "It's not going nowhere."

I nodded, unsure whether or not I was supposed to laugh.

Grandpa said something I couldn't hear to Max, who went to the garage, came back with a bottle of liquid and, under Grandpa's direction, began rubbing it on the chrome.

"They started going through Aloise's things," she said after a while, nodding toward Max and Grandpa. "I guess they don't need my help. Nobody asked for my help. Which is just fine by me."

I didn't know what to say, though I felt she was waiting for some sort of assurance.

"You like your grandpa?" she said suddenly.

I squirmed. "I guess so," I said uneasily. "He's my grandpa."

She took another long drag on her cigarette.

"He don't like me much."

I wanted to assure her that wasn't so, but instead I said, "How come?"

She flicked ashes from her cigarette, pulled something from her bottom lip with her long fingernails. They were painted mauve, like the eyeshadow.

"I just hope he don't want to palm that junk off on me," she said. "I don't have nowhere to put it. I'm moving into a new place and there's nowhere to put it."

And I remembered, then, that hairbrush I'd found months ago in the kitchen drawer at Uncle Aloetius' house.

"Isn't it your stuff?" I said. "Doesn't some of that stuff belong to you?"

She snorted but said nothing.

"I mean," I ventured, "you're still married to him. After all."

She peered at me, not in an angry way, just looking, then dropped her cigarette on the step and crushed it with her sandal.

"They don't divorce," she said, lifting her chin toward Grandpa. "They don't believe in it."

"Oh," I said again.

"I just say I'm widowed. That's what I've been saying all this time. I'm a widow." She shrugged. "So? Now I am one."

We sat there listening to the swish and rub of those rags across the Buick, Max and Grandpa working without speaking.

"I found a brush one time," I said after a while. "I thought maybe it was yours. It was blue."

"Maybe," she said. "I guess so. I guess it must've been mine."

"Don't you want it?"

"No," she said.

The sun was up full and hot, and I heard Grandma call breakfast from the kitchen window. Aunt Gerri looked as if she was going to rise, then stopped.

"Love," she began, and nodded. I waited for her to go on, but she just stared across the yard, at Max and Grandpa and the old Buick, at the cottonwood tree that needed to be cut down. I waited, with the sun hot on my knees. "Love," she repeated finally. "You think that's what it'll all be about. But then you find out, it is. Only not the way you thought." Then she nodded again and went inside.

IX

After the funeral, Aunt Gerri drove back to Medicine Hat and flew from there to Thunder Bay. She took nothing with her from Uncle Aloetius' house, nothing that I knew of anyway, though I thought she should at least have that picture of herself from Uncle Aloetius' bedroom. If I'd had the guts, I'd have gone over to get it for her. That and the hairbrush. But I didn't. That much, at least, had not changed.

I was the last one to see her before she left. I was sitting under the willow outside the church. Everyone else had already walked over to the community hall for the lunch the town ladies always provided after a funeral. Aunt Gerri came out the side door of the church, and I was about to call over to her when she stopped abruptly and leaned with one hand against the wall, as though dizzy. It was only a second, but I stood in alarm. Then she straightened and walked briskly to her car, her purple high heels clicking on the concrete. I knew she had seen me, but she did not look back, and I didn't blame her, not really. She just climbed into her car and, in a moment, was gone.

I was not surprised when I learned later that Uncle Aloetius had left her what little money he had. But it reminded me of what Grandpa had said about her. That she took money from a man not even—what? I never did find out, though I thought I knew. I thought it had something to do with love.

Max and Grandpa weren't around much in the days following; they spent most of their time across town, sorting through things, packing up all that junk or maybe throwing it away.

My grandmother said to me one afternoon as I stood by myself, kicking at the nearly dried cornstalks in the garden, "Why don't you go on over?" But we both knew I couldn't.

I crunched a browning stalk under my bare heel. "Why doesn't Grandpa like Aunt Gerri?" I asked.

Grandma smiled a little. "It's been so long," she said, "I don't think he remembers."

She bent and began collecting garden refuse in fistfuls, stuffing it into the plastic garbage bag she toted by her side.

"But you remember," I said.

Grandma stood up, laughed. "No." She shook her head. "Some things, it's best to let them go. Old hurts. Your grandpa

can't let go." She propped her hands on her hips and looked
with dismay around the garden, as if she'd only just noticed it,
the soft, yellowing leaves, the rusting, wrinkled flesh of pump-
kins. "Such a waste," she said. The thing she seemed to hate
above all.

"Do you like her?"

"I don't know her," she said.

I nodded, though her answer wasn't entirely satisfying.

"What will they do with his stuff?" I asked.

Grandma shrugged. "Keep it, I guess, his personal things.
There's room in the attic. See if your father wants anything."
She paused. "Is there anything you want?"

There was—of course there was.

"No," I said.

Grandma went back to gathering cornstalks. "Anyway," she
said, "we could all blame someone if we let ourselves. We all
have something we could blame someone for. But what's the
point?"

I felt bad, standing there watching while she worked, and so
I bent to help her.

"No," she said firmly. "I want to do this myself. If you want
to help, you can get me some more garbage bags from the
kitchen."

So I went, taking my time. I took the bags from the cupboard below the sink, then, thinking she might appreciate it,
went to the fridge to get her a cold drink. There on the bottom
shelf stood the bowl of saskatoons Max and I had picked the
day Aunt Gerri arrived. In all the upheaval, I'd forgotten
about the berries entirely, though Grandma had washed them
and put them in one of her good porcelain bowls. They lay
like dark pearls, beautiful now out of context, like something
of sand and water. It was almost a shock to find them among

the ordinariness of pickles and mayonnaise and eggs. I stood admiring them, just for a moment, and I thought, I'll remember this. I'll remember this one good thing.

Lillie

I

Lucy Satterley was sunbathing again, her hair pulled up in a knot on top of her head and secured with a ribbon the exact green of her two-piece swimsuit. She did not move, but every so often the wind would lift a long end of the ribbon in a cool, shimmering flap and twist it gaily about her ears, then let it fall. From where he sat in the shade on the low cinder-block wall, Owen, who was almost eight, noticed she'd slipped the straps of her swimsuit down over her shoulders, exposing a white, shining rim of flesh. She looked, he thought, like a water queen, like something you read of in books, some fine thing washed in from the sea. He mouthed her name, counting the beats off on his fingers: Lu-cy-Sat-ter-ley, Lu-cy-Sat-ter-ley. Five beats exactly, five fingers. It wasn't much of a game. He jumped down, brushed dust from the seat of his corduroy pants, waited a moment to see if she'd turn and notice him. When she didn't, he crossed the Satterleys' backyard to where she stretched belly-up on a silver blanket, glistening like a new fish. Owen sniffed. Up close, her skin had an oilier sheen and a smell like the cookies his mother used to bake—raisins and coconut. And something else, something like mown grass after it has lain for a while in the heat. He stood there, shifting his weight from foot to foot, willing her to move. A meadowlark sounded from down the alley. The ribbon danced briefly and fell. Finally, he peeled off his shirt, spread it on the lawn and sat down with his back to the sun, precisely, so that his shadow fell true to the line of his body.

Lucy did not move. He stared at the side of her head.

"Sure is hot," he said, plucking a blade of grass. He thought maybe she twitched, just a little, so he repeated himself, louder, and added conversationally, "Hotter'n a cat's snatch."

She rolled her head slowly toward him, opened one blue eye. For some reason, he had known she would have blue eyes, cool and transparent as rainwater.

"Where'd you hear that?" she drawled.

Her voice startled him a little. "Nowhere. I can just tell. It's hot, isn't it?"

"I mean 'cat's snatch.' Where'd you hear that?"

He shrugged, looked down at the grass. Something in her tone made him wish he had not come over after all.

"You shouldn't say that." She shifted her hips on the blanket. "It's not nice." She opened the other eye and peered at him sharply. "I bet you don't even know what that is."

Owen squinted up at a thick band of clouds ballooning toward them across the sky. Who cared if he didn't? He knew a lot of things. He knew it had not rained in forty-seven days. He kept track on a calendar his mother got from the bar. It had pictures of prairie scenes to match the seasons. Lucy humphed at his silence, but gently, like the sound a sleeping seal might make. Like the sound of those clouds moving. Fat with rain. Where did it go, that rain? If not here, where?

He knew by the rustle of her head brushing the silver blanket that she'd turned away again.

"It's hot anyways," he said after a while. He looked back at her, noticing how the sun lit the fine yellow hairs at the base of her head, how it left bluish shadows, like caves, behind her shoulders, under her arms. From the wall, he had longed to tickle her there, but now he could see this would not be possible. "I'm getting a new bike," he said, then felt foolish. Why would she care? "For my birthday," he added, but without conviction now. "Maybe."

He sighed and looked around the yard. There were three patches of petunias, purple and white, along the back of the house, and a big lilac tree with the blooms already gone to seed. There was a small aluminum shed, the kind people used to store lawn mowers and snow shovels and red plastic jerry cans. There was a garden hose curled through the dusty grass like a garter snake and a clay pot with three pink geraniums and, wedged far back under the steps, a cardboard box of glass bottles. There was a potato chip bag blown up against the cotoneaster hedge, but so low you couldn't see it unless you were sitting on the ground. There was a clothesline. And under the big shushing cottonwood at the back, there was a small table and two lawn chairs, the kind you could stretch out on. Beyond that, he knew, there was nothing. A few more houses, fields. The highway. And then the Sand Hills, barely visible. He often walked out to the eastern edge of town, just as far as the highway, and stared. People passing in cars and trucks stared back. Sometimes they waved.

"This morning," he began tentatively, "there were mirages on the highway."

Lucy squinted back at him, scowling.

"You know," he said, "like when you're driving down the highway and you see those big puddles of water, like the road is flooded out? But they disappear before you get there? That's a mirage."

"Yeah?" she said flatly.

"It's an optical illusion. Because the ground is hotter than the air. It's just the reflection of the sky getting *refracted*." He stressed the word, knowing he was showing off. Why not? "Refracted by the hot air on the ground. That's why it looks blue."

"Mmm." She turned her face away, toward the hedge.

"It works the other way around, too," he said loudly, "if the ground is cold and the air is warm. Like in winter. That's why sometimes it seems like things are closer than they really are. Like farms. Or towns." He leaned over her a little, to see if her eyes were open. They weren't. "Sometimes it looks like the Sand Hills are just on the other side of the highway. Like you could walk right over. You ever seen that?"

He wondered if he should explain about refraction, about how you could see it by holding a pencil in a glass of water. Probably she already knew about that.

"Anyway," he sighed, slumping back on the grass, "that's a mirage."

He watched the ribbon flip and settle. She was beginning to look a little pink. Hot. Had she fallen asleep?

"I can fill that spray bottle with ice water," he said. "My mom keeps a pitcher cold."

Lucy lay there motionless, her skin gleaming. Beads of sweat glinted in the hollow of her collarbone, like sparks, as though she would burst into flame at any second. It could happen. Spontaneous combustion.

Finally she said, "She home?"

What difference did that make? "No," he lied.

Without opening her eyes, she unscrewed the cap, dumped the tepid water from the Windex bottle on the grass at the edge of the blanket and held it out to him.

He eased himself up, noticing how his shadow fell across her belly in a wide, dark stripe. He wondered how long he would have to stand there in order to leave the white shape of his body on her skin. He banged the empty bottle against his leg a couple of times. Lucy opened her eyes.

"You want a drink?" he asked. "I could get something."

"Yeah," she said, "see if you got any Tang."

Owen slammed through the screen door. His mother knelt on the kitchen floor in a halter top and the cut-off shorts she wore to work, trimming new strips of MACtac to line the cupboards—yellow with green dots a shade lighter than Lucy's swimsuit. She was wearing the belt he hated, the one with her name stitched on the back, *Lillie.* He had one, too, in a box somewhere in the basement. *Owen.* Like it meant something. It was too small now. He'd picked them both out that year they'd gone together to the Stampede in Medicine Hat. He'd ridden on the carousel and on a pony, a brown one with big white patches that made him think of continents. And then she'd taken him on the Ferris wheel, and the wheel had stopped when they were almost right at the top, and he was amazed that even from way up there he could still smell red candied apples, like cinnamon, and popcorn and hotdogs (and mustard, he was sure he could smell mustard), and he wondered whether he just thought he could smell it because he knew it was all there, hamburgers and pizza and fat pink wads of cotton candy, and before he knew it the wheel had started, and they were at the bottom again, and his mother was holding the bar back so he could climb out, and he realized with dismay that he'd never even looked at the city. *How about a corn dog?* his mother said then. But he wasn't hungry. So they splurged—that's what his mother said—and bought the belts. Owen picked them out and stood watching while a man with an electric tool like a drill etched their names on the leather. He wished now he'd chosen something else. He wished his mother would not wear hers anymore, but he could not tell her this.

"Shush," she said as he stood in the kitchen doorway, though he had not said anything, "I just put the baby down." She leaned back on her haunches and frowned at him. "Owen. Where's your shirt?"

"I been in the shade," he said, trying not to look at the loose flesh of her belly over the shorts.

"Still." She put down the scissors. "Sun goes right through leaves, right through to your skin. You'll get sunstroke. Or skin cancer. Do you want that, skin cancer?"

Owen did not want skin cancer. He wished she would not say those things. He crossed the narrow kitchen and reached for two plain bar glasses from the shelf, then exchanged them for tall, clear mugs ringed with yellow sunflowers. He looked back at his mother. Would she say something about that?

"Dinner'll be ready soon," she said. Owen looked at the clock. It was after three. "Take some crackers if you're hungry," she added, "but use a paper plate, not the good patterned ones."

Owen took two pitchers from the refrigerator, poured both mugs almost full of Tang and filled the Windex bottle with cold water.

"Who's that for?" his mother asked, standing up and, almost in one motion, leaning into a chair. "Oh, my back. Sweetie, come and rub right here. Who's the Tang for?"

Owen dug his thumbs under his mother's shoulder blades. He could tell by her voice she was having a bad day. That was what she called them, her bad days.

"Just a friend."

"What friend?"

"Lucy."

"Lucy Satterley?" She frowned over her shoulder. "Lower, sweetie."

He shifted his hands down his mother's back, noticed a pinched red welt where the elastic of her top dug into her flesh. There seemed to be a lot of people his mother didn't want him to talk to. He hoped she would not say he couldn't talk to Lucy.

"You'd think I was eighty the way my back hurts. That's what a pregnancy'll do to you. That and worse. A bit to the right. The right."

Owen shifted his hands again, noticed some dirt under his fingernails, not much.

"With you, I couldn't hardly do nothing. Just lie around all day. Watch TV. Sometimes I'd do the hide-a-words, but . . ." She waved her hand.

Through the screen door, they could hear a dog begin to bark down the alley. Fletcher's dog, Boone. She never barked as if she was angry or excited. She just barked. It was something to do. Owen knew it would likely last all afternoon, perfectly measured, like the ticking of a clock.

Owen's mother raised her head, pushed her hair back from her forehead.

"Damn dog," she said.

Owen paused to flex his fingers.

"What did you say Lucy Satterley's doing here? Did her mom send her?"

"No," Owen said. "I was just talking to her. Over the wall."

"Oh." She straightened her shoulders, rolled her neck. "That's enough, sweetie. Those Satterleys," she said. "June borrowed my good cake pan last spring." She picked a piece of dried grass from Owen's pants. "Probably never see that again." She stood, rolling the grass between her fingertips. "Owen," she said after a moment, "how old is Lucy anyway?"

Owen took the plastic ice cube tray from the freezer, twisted it and pried out the cubes with his fingers.

"Must be in junior high now," she said. She stood there at the sink, lips pursed as if calculating. "Is she in junior high, Owen?"

"I dunno." He plunked two cubes in each glass and returned the tray to the freezer.

"Owen . . ." she said.

Owen paused, one hand on the freezer.

"You should put the ice in first," she said. "You splashed all over the counter." She stared at him a moment, then turned away, sighed. "Looks like rain." She tapped her fingernails on the counter, staring out the screen door.

It was what she always said. It was what everyone said. It would look as if rain was coming, but the clouds would just slide by. "Probably not," Owen said.

"No." She smiled a little. "Probably not."

Past her, he could see the roof of the school and beyond that, the tall black peak of St. Joseph's. He wondered whether Lucy had waited. His mother sighed again and knelt down by the MACtac. He could feel her watching as he filled a plate with graham crackers.

"You should put that on a tray, Owen," she said. "There's one in that box of kitchen stuff downstairs. The first one, I think, the big one."

He did not want a tray, but he was not willing to say this. He wanted to get back outside. What if she'd already gone into her house? It would be cloudy soon. She wouldn't stay out when it was cloudy.

Halfway down the stairs, Owen heard the baby howl. Would he have to stay in now? To help out? He pulled the string on the overhead bulb, poked around in the cardboard boxes in the corner, considering the possibility of mice, spiders. The floor creaked under his mother's weight above him, under the weight of the baby. He'd held it once. It weighed a lot, for something that size.

At the bottom of the second box, he found an old Pepsi-Cola tray, probably from the bar, too. It reminded him of last winter, when he'd had the flu. He'd spent nearly a week stretched out on the chesterfield in the front room, reading comic books while his mother brought him glass after glass of flat ginger ale on that tray. That had been a good week, in spite of the flu. Owen closed the box and headed for the stairs. As always when leaving the basement, he kept the light on, unwilling to turn his back on a darkened room.

Owen eased himself across the wall. Lucy had rolled onto her stomach and leaned on one elbow, looking at the Sears catalogue, her swimsuit straps dangling down over the pinkish tops of her arms.

"About time." Her face looked red and swollen from the heat. "What are you wearing those pants for? Aren't you godawful hot?"

He set the tray down carefully on the grass. She took one of the mugs and flipped a page in the catalogue. When he didn't answer, she looked up at him. "What you got to wear pants for?"

"Skin cancer," he said, before he could stop himself.

"You got skin cancer?"

He rubbed his palms on his pants. "Maybe."

"That'll kill ya, you know."

"I know."

She let the catalogue fall shut.

"I had a cousin died last summer," she said. "Brain

aneurysm. Popped off in the middle of the night and nobody knew nothing about it. Ten years old. Just like that." She snapped her fingers. "Found her in the morning and it looked like she was sleeping." Lucy took a bite of graham cracker and added ominously, "Only she wasn't." She paused to brush crumbs from her lips. "Maybe you got a brain aneurysm."

"No," he said, "I don't."

"You better hope not." She reached for another cracker. "You better hope it's not a brain aneurysm. They get you in your sleep. Just like that. You might have one. You wouldn't know it if you did, and then one night—" She snapped her fingers again.

"I don't have an aneurysm," Owen said irritably, poking at the ice cubes in his glass.

"How do you know?"

"My mom would know. She'd know."

"She'd know it when she found you laid out stone-cold dead in the morning, that's what." Lucy finished the crackers and closed her eyes, resting her head on her folded arms. Owen could see fine bits of graham cracker stuck to the sweat above her lip.

His mother would know. Of course she would. Even with the baby. She'd know. He thought about what she'd said as he was leaving: "You tell that Lucy Satterley—" Then she'd shaken her head, jiggled the baby against her chest. "Remind Lucy her mother has my good baking pan." She wouldn't let something like that happen to him, something like an aneurysm. But he did not want to talk to Lucy about his mother. He did not want to talk about her at all. He thought of what they said sometimes at school, chanting it during recess but quietly so the teachers wouldn't hear, *Lillie Gower ain't no flower.* It was stupid. And it wasn't the worst thing they said, not by far. But it made him angry anyway. Lucy would never say that. Or would she?

He looked up at the sky, at the fat clouds moving heavily. Soon they would be right overtop of them.

"My mom wants her baking pan," he blurted.

"What?"

"My mom wants her baking pan."

"Right now?"

"Yes." He stuck out his chin. "She's baking a cake." He sat up straight and added, "Not for the baby."

"I thought you said she wasn't home."

Lucy clucked her tongue against her teeth and sat up, the top of her swimsuit dipping low across her chest, the skin there mapped with the creases of the silver blanket. Owen stared at the white rim of flesh. It was the prettiest thing. Like the inside of a seashell.

"What are you looking at?" she demanded. "You little perv." She didn't move to pull the straps up.

"I'm not a perv."

"Yes, you are. Perv." She smirked, leaning forward. "Snatch."

Owen stood up, brushed the grass from his knees and pulled his shirt on. The sun had made him dizzy, and he wobbled a bit as he bent for the tray.

"I'm not finished yet," Lucy said, grabbing her mug. She tilted her head back and drained the mug, exposing the sweat-streaky white flesh of her neck and chest. Letting her top slip down so he could see the smooth tops of her breasts. He looked quickly away.

"Thanks," she said as she handed him the mug, sucking on an ice cube wedged in the corner of her mouth. "Perv."

II

Lucy'd seen Lillie Gower's kid straddling the wall long before he'd finally jumped down and come over. She'd known it was just a matter of time; he'd sat there every day this week. She hadn't seen him around much since they'd moved in last fall, wouldn't have known him from Adam if she'd passed him on the street. But she knew Lillie. Everybody did. The kid had her build, real small-boned. And that hair, not quite blond, not quite brown. Sort of cardboard-coloured.

She looked back at him through the sliding glass doors. He stood in the middle of the yard, hands jammed deep in the pockets of those ridiculous pants. Who would dress their kid like that in this heat? He turned toward the house then, shading his eyes, and she stepped away from the doors. Maybe she shouldn't have done that, flashed him that way. It wasn't really like her. There was just something about the way he'd kept gawking, thinking she didn't even notice. Something sly.

Still, with a mother like that, the kid was bound to be a little weird. A cocktail waitress, at her age, in those skimpy shorts, two kids later. Who was she kidding? She must be at least thirty. No, was she that old? She didn't really look it, not in the face, not really. It was hard to tell. Lucy had seen her up close only that one time, in the alley outside the bar. And it had been dark, with just the yellow bulb over the back door. And Lucy had drunk the beer that Rick's cousin had snuck out for him under his jacket. When she thinks about that night, she can still taste the beer. Awful. It had made her eyes water. But she'd drunk it anyway, tried to guzzle it to make it go down fast. And Rick had grabbed her, laughing, falling against her into the wall. And the cousin, laughing, too, cracking open another beer. *This one's on Lillie.*

Bullshit, Rick had said, *you're full of shit.*

I'm not shitting you, man.

Shit, Rick said, shaking his head. *So what're you doing here?*

And the cousin grinned, stepping back into the bar, Rick laughing.

And she had laughed, too, though she hadn't found anything particularly funny, and she remembered there was glass under her shoes, she could hear it crunching, and she was scared it might punch right through her runners into her foot. She'd heard about that, about people stepping on rusty nails or dirty glass, so she'd pushed Rick backwards a little, just to get away from it. She didn't know why he got so mad then, shoving her back up against the wall. She'd knocked her head on the bricks, but it hadn't hurt, not really. And for a minute she'd thought it was all right, of course it was, this was just Rick. Only she was crying. She was dizzy and crying and her sweater was off and tangled somewhere down in the dirt. She was freezing, with glass under her feet and all that yellow light like stars falling, and then Lillie was right there, trashy Lillie Gower who wore her shorts too short and her hair too big. Her face was up against Lucy's, so close Lucy could smell her gum, peppermint, and Rick was running down the alley with his cousin. Lillie was draping the sweater across Lucy's chest, saying, *You okay, sweetie, you okay?* over and over, her face soft in that light and shifting, like sand.

And that's when she'd been sick. Lillie had her by the shoulder, saying, *Stay here, I'll get you some water. Stay right here.* And she had slipped into the door below the yellow bulb, a blast of laughter and music blowing out behind her. Before she could come back, Lucy'd wiped her chin with her sweater and run down the alley toward home, tripping against the ruts, wondering if Rick would be there waiting for her, half hoping he would be. He wasn't, though. She hadn't seen him since, except that one afternoon down at Boyle's. But he was paying for a Coke and didn't see her walk by.

She'd almost expected Lillie to show up, too, the next day, maybe say something to her mother. She hadn't, of course— they weren't friends or anything, her mother and Lillie. Anyway, Lillie Gower wasn't anybody to be afraid of.

And now here was her kid, leering at Lucy in the backyard.

She pulled the blinds shut and headed for the kitchen. It was freezing. Her mother must be home, pumping the air conditioning again. The house was never the right temperature, cold in the summer, hot in the winter. She grabbed her dad's old gardening cardigan from a hook by the back door and pulled it on over her swimsuit.

"Mom," she shouted. "Lillie Gower wants her cake pan." She could hear the low hum of a radio on somewhere above. "Mom!" she hollered up the dim stairs. And waited.

"For Jesus' sake," she grumbled, banging up the carpeted steps in her bare feet. She'd catch hell for that; there was probably grass all over them. "Mom," she said, swinging open her mother's bedroom door, "Lillie Gower wants her cake pan."

Her mother was sitting in an armchair by the window, looking out at the backyard, a romance novel spine-up on her leg. "Yes," she said, turning around, "I heard."

Lucy pulled the cardigan across her stomach. Had her mother been sitting by the window the whole time? She fingered the ribbon on top of her head.

Her mother sat with her legs crossed, the pale blue housewrap she always wore on Sundays draped neatly to her ankles. She stared at Lucy, then clicked off the radio that was playing softly on the nightstand.

Lucy rubbed her arms. "Does it have to be forty below in here?"

"Is that Owen down there?" her mother asked, turning back to the window. Lucy shifted her feet. Well, so what? She hadn't really done anything. Besides, her mother should take care of her own problems. She noticed the glass tumbler beside the radio, empty.

Her mother rose then and stepped into the adjoining bathroom, closing the door. Lucy crossed the room quietly, sniffed the empty glass. Water or vodka, she couldn't tell for sure. She tilted the glass back to her mouth. Water. She set it carefully back down over its wet ring.

In the yard below, Owen had moved into the shade, sitting with his shirt on, the Pepsi tray balanced on his knees, staring up at the sky, motionless. Beyond the yard, she could see the highway and then the yellow glint of the Sand Hills. Looking just as they always did, rising up in gentle ridges from the horizon like the backs of whales. She hadn't ever noticed that they looked closer in winter. And how did he know all that stuff anyway? Probably he'd made it up.

Her mother came back in a loose white sundress.

"I'm sure I returned that."

"What?"

"That cake pan. I'm sure I returned it ages ago."

Lucy stretched the cardigan down over her thighs. Jesus, it was freezing. "What'd you borrow a cake pan of Lillie Gower's for anyway?"

Her mother smoothed her skirt, checked the hem. "Does she need it right now? I suppose so. Or she wouldn't have sent Owen."

"So he says." Lucy turned back to the window, looked down at Owen. What was he staring at? "Is he sick?" she asked.

"Who?"

"Owen Gower."

"Is he?" Her mother misted her throat with a spray bottle from the dresser. "Not that I know of. Why do you ask?"

"Just wondering." Lucy leaned on the window ledge, stared down at her legs. She did have grass on her feet. She brushed it off against the carpet. "He *says*"—she drew the word out—"he says he's got skin cancer."

Lucy's mother laughed. "I don't think Owen Gower has skin cancer."

Below them, Owen had not moved. Geez, that kid was patient. Lucy put a finger up on the glass, right over his small body. She could block him out completely if she wanted to.

"Don't smear that, Lucy," her mother said.

Lucy moved her finger, looked down at Owen, at his small, pale face turned up to the sky. She shouldn't have flashed him like that. She picked up the empty glass on the table, watched her mother slip into a pair of sandals.

"Where you going?"

"To take the cake pan back."

Lucy put the glass down, stared at her mother. "That's what he's here for," she said. "He's down there waiting. You can't just send him home, after he's been waiting like that."

"Oh, I should probably stop by and see that baby."

"What for?" Lucy said. She wasn't chilly anymore, she felt her body flush, from the stomach upward. Her head began to ache. "You don't even know her." Maybe she'd stayed out in the sun too long. "Send it back with him."

"What's the matter with you?"

Lucy turned toward the window.

"You don't even know her," she said. She closed her eyes, rubbed her temples. Thought of Owen sitting below her on the grass. Of Lillie, her face so round and soft under the yellow light. She wasn't anybody to be afraid of. She was just Lillie Gower. A cocktail waitress. A barmaid. She was trash.

"Lucy," her mother said, stepping toward her in a hot cloud of lilac perfume, "what in the world are you crying about?"

Redberry,
Ministikwan,
Buffalo Pound

For the second time that morning, Lavinia left her spade and the pails of potatoes she'd been digging to slip between the tight rows of corn standing blue and hard in the early light. She pulled off her coat—one of Jack's old flannel ones, far too large—and wiped sweat from her forehead and upper lip with the hem of her shirt. She leaned back, resting her forehead against her arms, and tried to take long, slow breaths, tried to pull the air through her, clear and cold and still-dark, like water from the rain barrel when the ice was chipped open. It would be good to go there now, to where it stood under the shadows of the eaves on the north side of the house, hack off a big chunk to hold between her lips. But Jack would think she was slacking. So she crouched between the rows of corn, smelling the rich root-cellar smell of dug potatoes and rolling her forehead against the skin of her arms.

From where she crouched, she could see Jack through the browning leaves, hammering against the truck engine by the barn, each blow ringing across the yard like the clipped pealing of a bell. It was a strange sound, one that did not travel up, toward the slowly lightening sky, but only outward, across the fields—still dark and rimy—as though it too stuck fast to the earth. Each blow running in ripples beneath her boots, shivering up through her bones, her stomach—a small, wayward earthquake.

That shivering made her think of those snake pits where she'd stopped once with her parents, on the only family holiday they'd ever taken—south, to Cypress Hills. They'd stood, the three of them, looking down at what appeared at first not to be snakes at all, but simply a shifting mass that rippled as though beneath one skin.

But once she'd been able to distinguish the individual bodies on the rocks, Lavinia could not look at them without a queasy, dizzy, skin-crawling feeling, as if she could sense their movements coming up through the earth to her feet. And so she'd tried to pretend she was somewhere else, staring instead at the sunlight beating off a tin sign she could not read in the distance, until her mother finally sighed, "We should get a move on, I guess," and her father said, "Road's not getting any shorter," and they'd piled into the car, Lavinia in the back, wedged in on one side by suitcases and a plastic cooler, panting and sick, forehead up against the hot window, unable, for some reason, to roll it down, to touch anything with her hands.

Just thinking of those snakes made her feel ill again, so she thought instead about earthquakes, about how the ground could split open in a second, swallowing everything. Not here, though. That kind of thing didn't happen here. No natural disasters, nothing quick and awful and spectacular. Just drought. Just slow death.

For two weeks now, she'd been feeling weak, tired—no, exhausted. "Strong as a horse," Jack used to boast when they were first married, "and twice as hungry." It was a stupid thing to say, but she'd liked it, heaping another helping onto her plate as if to say, *He's right, you see? I never fill up, I never do.* As if it united them somehow.

Now she could eat almost nothing; at times, she thought she could even feel something there in the pit of her stomach, something hard and foreign. Lump, she thought, and clenched her hands into cold fists against her belly. But there was no real pain. Not yet, anyway. Just a terrible sense of something gone wrong.

When Lavinia met Jack, she'd already lived in Medicine Hat a few years, city girl, sworn off ever returning to the dust hole where her parents still farmed. "A desert," she told the girls at the all-night pancake house where she worked, "right down to the damn dunes." And she'd describe the hills where her father grazed his cattle, the parched scrub, the hot smell of stinkweed and sage, the sandfly bites that would swell instantly to the size of quarters. She'd tell all the jokes she knew—*Hear about the hooker who entertained a farmer from Saskatchewan? How did she know he was from Saskatchewan? First it was too dry, then it was too wet, then he asked if he could pay her in fall.* She'd shake her head and say, "Wild horses."

Then Jack turned up. He came in one night with some friends, drunk, all of them, and rude. She'd cried afterwards, when she was alone in the staff bathroom. She wasn't sure why; she'd had worse customers. When he came back the next morning to apologize, she agreed—maybe because of the way he stood awkwardly at the till, waiting for her to finish her table, his plaid shirt so new she could still see the creases from the package; maybe because he used her name without checking the tag on her shoulder; or maybe just because, after all, he seemed awfully sincere—to go on a date with him.

She wasn't surprised to discover he was from the Sand Hills, too. Lots of people around town were, younger people, unwilling or unable to continue battling the land for a living. The struggle wasn't worth it. Farming wasn't about pride anymore, or love, and certainly not about money. Besides, there was plenty of work to be had in the oil patch. Big money. And you could travel. *Will the last person to leave Saskatchewan please turn out the lights?* That was the running joke. Lavinia never said it, though; that one she didn't find particularly funny.

Neither did Jack. "Ingrates," he said that first night as they sat over beers in the Westlander. "And smartasses. Not a clue what it took to get those farms started. What their grandparents went through. Great-grandparents. Stuck it out through the thirties and God knows what all kinds of hell." He shook his head. "Now? Too goddamn lazy. Spoiled. Got the world figured out."

He pulled a cigarette from the pack on the table, tapped it. Lavinia sipped her beer, thinking, He has the bluest eyes, blue like the lakes in the Wheat Pool calendars—photographs she'd clipped and Scotch-taped to the walls and ceiling of her bedroom when she was a girl, loving both the scenery and the names: Jackfish, Witchekan, Big Quill. She'd lie across her bed on hot summer afternoons and stare into all that blue, running the names cooly through her head, like a chant. Pelletier, Candle, Old Wives.

"Tell me," he said, pointing his cigarette at her, "tell me you don't miss it. All that open space. Those fields. The light there. Some days you can see ten, twelve miles."

That reminded Lavinia, briefly, of another joke, something about watching your dog run away for three days. But she did not tell it. She was listening to Jack, thinking, Maybe I wasn't looking, all those years. Maybe it was there. All that time. Maybe it was me.

Thinking, Bigstick, Manito, Willow Bunch.

Jack leaned toward her across the table, so close she could see those lakes had little yellowish pockets of light, shifting like water lilies. Like trout. "Tell me," he said again, "tell me you don't miss it."

Two weeks after the wedding, she packed up the few dishes and odd bits of furniture she'd collected, helped Jack load it all into his truck and they headed east, making a quick stop at the pancake house so Lavinia could drop off her uniform and pick up her final cheque.

"Never thought I'd see the day," one of the girls said.

"Yeah," Lavinia said. "Well."

She spent the first few months setting the old farmhouse in order—rearranging kitchen cupboards, sweeping out closets, even putting a row of petunias and marigolds in the freshly weeded patch beneath the south kitchen windows, carrying water to them in an old ice cream pail every evening.

Her mother was thrilled. "My daughter," she said, "come back to the fold."

Her father simply gloated. "Got yourself a nice place here," he'd say, looking around. "View of the Sand Hills." He'd say it each time they came.

And at first she kind of thought so, too. It was a nice place. The red-painted outbuildings, the neat white farmhouse which, though small, was bright and had a tiny veranda round the back where she could imagine them sitting on rare windless evenings, sipping coffee, listening to the crickets and watching the light slip off the land.

Now, a little more than a year later, they had yet to sit there in the companionable silence she had imagined. Jack, she realized, never ·sat. He just moved from one task to the next, evenly. When he stopped, he slept. Determined to make the best of it and to entice him, too, she'd tried sitting there one evening on her own, pulling out two kitchen chairs. But she felt guilty and then angry, watching him cross and re-cross the yard well into dusk. Ignoring her. Making his point. And so she'd dragged the chairs back inside, sat instead looking out the kitchen window where at least he could not see her. Sat looking at those red buildings slowly darken and sag. Wondering why she hadn't noticed before how they all seemed to tilt slightly in one direction from the constant assault of wind.

Homestead, he'd called the farm when they first met, a place he could not possibly leave. "They can put me six-feet-under right back by the barn. Suit me fine."

Homestead.

At the time, it had made sense to her. Such a beautiful word. Endearing. And she'd thought, quite stupidly, He could make me love it.

The ringing of the hammer against the truck engine stopped, and in a moment Lavinia heard Jack's heavy bootfalls coming across the yard. She wiped her face again, pulled on her coat and quickly slipped back through the leaves. But he was already standing there, her spade held loosely in his fingertips.

"I had to pee," she said, though there was no real reason why she should explain. He looked down at the near-empty bucket. "Ground's hard," she added. "On account of the frost."

She held out her hand for the spade, thinking he might drop it there in the dirt. It was hard to tell with Jack. Moody. But he just nudged the bucket with the toe of his boot and handed her the spade.

"Going to Schecters'," he said.

Lavinia had not been to Ray Schecter's place since that once before she and Jack were married, not long after Ray's wife had been taken back to the hospital in North Battleford for the third and possibly final time. Lavinia had never met her.

"She's a schizo," Jack had explained amiably as they rode over in the truck. "You know what that is, a schizo?" Before she could answer, he reached across and squeezed her thigh. "That's a schizophreniac." He tapped his forehead beneath his cap. "She's not right."

Lavinia plucked gently at the dark hairs on the back of his hand and he pulled it away. "What do you mean," she asked, "not right?"

He rolled the window down and adjusted the rear-view mirror, though there was nothing to see behind the truck but a cloud of dust. She turned anyway, just to check.

"She's mental. What more do you want to know?"

"I mean," she said, "how did it happen?"

"How should I know? She's a schizo. They're probably born that way."

Lavinia frowned and looked out the window, out over the brown furrows of fallow fields that looked as if they'd been raked by enormous fingers in smooth and continuous patterns. The familiar monotony of colour, the unvarying shape of the land. The way you could never get out of that sun, or that wind. It could make anyone crazy.

"What's the matter now?" Jack said.

"Nothing," she said carefully. "It's just, that doesn't sound nice, calling her that. A schizo. It sounds . . . disrespectful." But disrespectful was not what she meant. She did not know exactly what she meant, only that the word grated on her. *Schizo*.

"Oh, for Christ sakes." Jack shook his head, tipped the brim of his cap lower. They hit a particularly hard ridge on the dirt road (on purpose, Lavinia thought) and the truck jumped, jolting her on the seat so hard, her teeth clacked together.

Up ahead, Schecters' place sat neatly on a small rise, the house at the highest point, the outbuildings sloping gradually away, as if sliding almost imperceptibly downhill, though the word *downhill* was in itself a gross exaggeration.

"Anyway," Lavinia said, "it doesn't matter." She rested her hand on his arm.

"Okay," Jack said. "Okay. Forget it."

They rolled past the house, and Jack pulled the truck to a stop outside the hog pens. Ray was already there, leaning across the railings. Lavinia reached for the handle, but Jack said, "Won't be long," and slammed the door, crossing the yard in long strides.

Lavinia sat in the hot cab, feeling close to tears, Ray's presence a few yards away the only thing keeping them in check. Over nothing, she thought. That was the worst part.

She watched Ray look up as Jack approached, lift one hand in a half-greeting and lean back away from the pens, his T-shirt pushed up a little over his belly. He shook his head at Jack, jerked a thumb toward the pens. "Sonofabitch," he said, and shook his head again. She watched as Jack hooked his long body across the rails, then leaned back, too, tipping his cap away from his forehead. "I'll be goddamned," he said. Then he turned suddenly and waved to Lavinia. "Come on," he called.

Ray nodded at her as she stepped up to the pen.

"See that?" Jack said, pulling her close by the sleeve of her shirt.

At first she saw nothing but a large, spotted sow, curled sideways in the mud.

"What?" she said.

"There," Jack said, pulling her closer.

She leaned across the rails, peering over to where Jack pointed.

"Only one left," Jack said. "Christ, Ray, that's a goddamn shame."

It was the blood she noticed first, a rusty brown colour smeared across the sow's muzzle, then the one piglet squirming between its mother's speckled hind end and the pen boards.

"What?" she was about to say again, but Jack said, "Nature's way, I guess. It's a Christly shame, but there ain't much you can do about it."

"Nature's way," Ray said. "Shit."

Lavinia looked up at Jack, and as she did, realized with a terrible, heavy feeling in her stomach what they were talking about. She stepped back from the pen—lurched back, she knew, though neither Jack nor Ray seemed to notice. It was one of the things she found hardest of all, living there on the farm with Jack—getting used to the ugliness all over again, the blood and sudden deaths, the way a headless body could race oblivious, as if fleeing for its life. The smell of it all.

Ray took off his cap, slapped it against the rails. "Guess I should try and get that last one."

Jack shook his head. "Be a cold day in hell before you'd catch me in there. She'll chew your nuts off."

Ray put his cap back on and kicked a clump of mud from

the rails. "Yeah," Lavinia heard him say as she walked quickly back to the truck, "guess you're right."

She slammed the door and sat there in the cab, hot, thinking, You bastard. Why would you show me that? But she already knew.

Toughen her up. City girl.

She jammed her spade now into the dirt and rubbed her shirt between her breasts where a line of sweat trickled toward her belly. Her armpits were wet and itchy and had a rank, oniony smell, although she'd bathed the night before and dusted on talcum. She thought, with disgust, I am rotting from the inside out. Jack had noticed, too, rolling away from her last night and twitching into sleep. She'd lain there in the darkness, pressing the palms of her hands into her belly, willing the sickness away. She'd prayed a bit, too, a kind of Hail Mary, what she could remember of it. But she must have fallen asleep partway through because she didn't remember getting to the end. When she'd awoken, she'd thought, That's a sin. It must be. It must be worse to start a prayer and not finish than to never pray at all.

By the time Lavinia had filled a bucket, the sun was high and the frost had turned wet on the earth. Mud had caked to the spade and to her rubber boots. She was so thirsty, her tongue felt swollen and heavy in her mouth. When Jack left her standing in the corn, she'd watched for a while as his truck disappeared down the road. Then she removed her coat and shirt and worked in her bra. Though the air was still cold, sweat collected beneath her armpits, and even working slowly as she was, she was forced to sit frequently on an upturned bucket to rest. The surface of the earth was damp and soft, but underneath it was still clenched with frost and she had to stomp hard on the spade to gain even a couple inches of depth. She thought she might go back to the house, rest a while and then come out again when the earth had warmed. Jack would likely be at Schecters' all day, maybe that night as well. And she could always hear the truck coming anyway. She planted the spade into a mound of dirt and lugged the full pail to the house, stopping every few feet to rest.

The clock in the kitchen showed just shy of noon. She washed her face at the sink and rubbed it dry with a dish towel, then drank four mugs of water so fast it trickled from the corners of her mouth. Now, a few minutes on the couch was all she needed.

But once she lay down, she realized she could not sleep. She kept thinking for some reason about Ray, about his wife, trying to imagine what she looked like. She'd asked Jack once.

"Christ," he'd said, rubbing the back of his neck, "I don't know." He shrugged. "She's blonde."

"Pretty?"

"I don't know," he said again. "I guess so. In a way."

Lavinia could not imagine Ray with someone who was pretty. But as soon as she'd thought it, she felt bad.

"What's she like?"

"Christ, Lavinia, I don't know. What do you keep harping on her for all the time?"

"Just curious, I guess." Then she added, "He must miss her, living there all by himself."

"He goes to see her," Jack said. "He visits her. All the time."

Lavinia wanted to say, "Would you? If it were me, would you visit all the time?" but instead she said, "They didn't have kids?"

"Not that I know of."

She was about to ask, "Why not?" when Jack said, "Enough, already. I don't want to talk about her."

At the time, she hadn't thought it an odd thing to say. But later, she'd wondered about the intimacy of what he'd said. Not "I don't want to talk about it," but "I don't want to talk about *her*."

And she'd felt angry and embarrassed and unreasonably jealous. She knew it was stupid. Still, sometimes she thought about Ray's wife quite a bit, tried to picture her face, her hair. What shade of blonde? Long hair, or short?

Later, Lavinia sat wedged between Jack and Ray on the truck seat. Ray spread himself out, knees apart, one arm across the back of the seat behind her. They both reeked of sweat and liquor, but what was worse was that Lavinia could still smell her own rotting odour.

Jack was driving fast, swerving sometimes in the soft ridge of gravel at the shoulder. Lavinia clutched the edge of the seat, wishing she'd learned how to drive a standard, dizzy and hot, sick with the careening motion, the smell of them all, bumping against each other at every jolt and turn. She wished she had stayed home, but that would not have been possible. Jack was in high spirits when he and Ray returned from Ray's place that evening, jovial. He would have coaxed, cajoled and, finally, become annoyed with her if she'd refused. Besides, getting out now and then wasn't so bad. It was just this nausea. And the thirst. She wished she'd brought something to drink. She wished a lot of things.

Jack fiddled with the radio, found the country station he liked.

"So," Ray hollered over the music, leaning in too close to her ear, "ever been to a carnival before?"

"No," she said, turning slightly away from the sour yeast smell of his breath.

"You gonna keep that to yourself, you miser?" Jack eyed the bottle wedged between Ray's thighs.

Ray passed it across her, banging his elbow accidentally into her mouth as they hit a pothole. She rubbed her tongue across the inside of her lip, could taste a bit of blood where the skin was ragged.

"I've been to a few," Ray said, oblivious. "Been to that fair in Saskatoon, too, the big one."

Jack took a long drink from the bottle, passed it back to Ray. "You never been out of this county in your life."

Lavinia looked at him quickly, thinking, His wife's in North Battleford. He goes there all the time. You said.

Ray tried to manoeuvre the bottle to his mouth but kept getting jolted, his arm flailing in mid-air. Rye splashed out on Lavinia's sleeve. "In sixty-eight," he hollered. "Before I was married." He screwed the lid clumsily back onto the bottle. "Was something else."

Lavinia shifted her weight on the seat, reached behind to adjust the sharp end of a seat belt clip that was digging into her back. She would have liked to put the belt on, but there was no way to do it without their noticing. She thought, If I have to die, don't let me die like this. Not in a graceless twist of metal.

"There was a woman, I swear to God, a woman weighed over nine hundred pounds."

Jack laughed and thumped the wheel.

"And one," Ray said, encouraged, "half-man, half-woman. She had a beard. And—you know. Everything."

Lavinia thought Jack would laugh again, but he just shook his head. "Christ," he said.

"And there was this thing," Ray said. "Hell, I don't remember what they called it. It was, well, it was human, I guess—part, anyway—but they kept it in this cage, and they warned everybody, 'Keep your hands away from the bars!' Didn't have to tell me twice. Bit the heads off live chickens."

"No shit," Jack said.

"No," Ray answered, settling back against the seat. "No shit."

Lavinia looked at him quickly. Something about his voice had made her think, with a start, He's faking. He's not drunk at all. And she wondered, Is he so lonely, then? Is he that desperate?

Jack suddenly pulled the truck to the side of the road. "Gotta see a man about a horse," he said.

When they were alone, Lavinia, on impulse, turned to Ray. "What's her name, anyway, your wife?"

"Linda," he said, his voice sounding startled in the dark of the cab.

"You must miss her," she said.

But before he could answer, Jack swung the door open and slid in beside her, singing, "My Bucket's Got a Hole in It."

When neither she nor Ray joined in, he whistled the song to himself, tapping his fingers against the steering wheel. The three of them shoulder to shoulder, Jack hurtling them through the darkness, toward the lights of town.

The carnival wasn't as big as Lavinia expected. They'd set up in the empty lot by the railroad tracks across from the bar. Cars lined both sides of the street for blocks—farmers and people who'd come from other places where the carnival wasn't stopping—but most of the town people just walked down. They strolled every street, ghostly and bristling with excitement.

Jack took one last swig of rye and led them to where two torches marked the entrance. Lavinia and Ray trailed slightly behind. She glanced over at him once, at the heavy set of his shoulders, and thought he wanted her to say something to him. Something, maybe, about his wife. But Jack turned to wait for them, so she hitched her purse strap up and kept walking.

"What's the matter?" Jack said, thumping Ray on the shoulder. "Somebody can't hold their liquor?"

Ray laughed a little and nodded. "I'll get it," he said, as they reached the gate. He paid for all three tickets and handed them their stubs. Then they stood there a moment, looking around.

"Hey," Jack said to Ray, "there's your girlfriend." He pointed at a garishly painted sign depicting a bearded lady. "Let's see if she still remembers you."

Ray nodded and jingled some change loosely in his pocket. "I need to take a leak," he said abruptly.

"Suit yourself," Jack said as Ray disappeared into the crowd. "Guess you're not interested," he said to Lavinia.

She shook her head, but he had already wandered off across the field, bumping into people as he went. Lavinia looked past the booths to where a lighted Ferris wheel turned slowly against the sky. She walked toward it through the bright alley made by the food vendors, realizing for the first time that she hadn't eaten yet that day. She positioned herself in line at the first vendor and ordered a Coke and two hotdogs, eating the first immediately in three huge bites while standing at the booth, then downing half the Coke. It was possible, she realized, that she hadn't eaten in days. Maybe that was the problem. Maybe she wasn't sick at all. She took the second hotdog and her Coke and strolled back toward the Ferris wheel. It was darker there, away from the food. And cooler. She felt better than she had in weeks.

"Ma'am," someone said, close to her. Lavinia started, almost dropped the half-eaten hotdog she held. She realized she'd been expecting Ray, but the man at her elbow was young, a teenager probably. A boy. His hair combed back slick from his scarred face.

"Ma'am," he said, smiling, "you have not seen nothing till you have seen the eighth wonder of the world, and we have it right here." He waved toward a small trailer at his back, lit by a single yellow bulb. "Right on up those stairs, ma'am, is a sight to behold straight from the Amazon jungles, the only one of its kind in captivity."

"What is it?" she asked, unable to look away from the fine fuzz of hair that darkened his upper lip. He had an accent. American.

"What is it, ma'am?" the boy repeated and then leaned in confidentially. "It is the giant anaconda of the Amazon jungle, measuring thirty-two feet long. That's right, thirty-two feet."

Lavinia looked over her shoulder toward the bearded lady tent. She couldn't see Jack or Ray anywhere, but it was difficult in this crowd. "How much?" she asked the boy, wiping a spot of mustard from the corner of her mouth.

"Just fifty cents," he said, "and worth every penny."

She handed the boy her Coke while she rummaged in her purse for some change.

"That's right," the boy called to people passing them, "straight from the Amazon jungles."

She slipped two quarters in his palm, took her Coke and headed up the steps.

"Whoops," the boy said to her, tapping the hotdog, "you can't take that in there."

Lavinia considered throwing it away, but instead she hungrily stuffed the whole thing in her mouth. As she turned to drop the wrapper into the garbage, she saw someone moving far on the other side of the trailer, past the lights, near the chain-link fence at the tracks. It looked like Ray. And she thought, Is it possible she's really never coming home, his wife? And then something else occurred to her, something she'd never thought to ask Jack, about Ray's wife going back to the hospital, maybe forever: Who decided?

The man at the fence—was it Ray?—looked over then and Lavinia waved. She was about to call out to him when the boy ushered her inside along with a couple she didn't recognize. The woman held a little girl by the hand. "Excuse me," she said politely as they squeezed by Lavinia in the doorway.

Inside, the trailer was smaller than it had appeared and completely dark except for a flat lighted cage in the centre of the room. The man held the little girl up so that she could see inside.

"That doesn't look like thirty-two feet, does it, Harv?" said the woman.

"Say," the man said to the boy who had followed them in, "this snake isn't thirty-two feet."

"That's the thing," the boy said, "it's hard to tell when they're all balled up like that. But see down there, that's the tail. Imagine, now, if it was all stretched out."

The woman looked skeptical. "Still," she said, "thirty-two feet."

Lavinia moved closer, looked in at the snake. The woman was right, it didn't really look that big. It lay motionless, a dull grey colour.

"Daddy," the little girl said, "doesn't it do anything?"

"Well?" the man demanded of the boy who leaned in behind Lavinia, pressing against her, smelling of peppermint candy. "Doesn't it do anything?"

"A snake this size," he said, "they don't move around much."

The woman made a *tsk* sound with her tongue against her teeth. "Well," she said, "that's not very interesting."

"No," the boy agreed, "no, you're absolutely right. But I'll show you something that is."

"What's he going to do, Daddy?" the little girl asked as the boy returned with a small cardboard box.

"I'll tell you what," the boy said to her, "would you like to help me give this old snake her supper?"

The little girl nodded and the mother said, "Oh, aren't you lucky now."

"I don't know." The man hesitated, looking from his wife to his daughter. "Is this such a good idea?"

"Why, sure." The boy grinned. "It's nature."

He removed the lid from the cardboard box.

"Okay," the boy said, "I don't do this for just anybody."

The little girl looked up at Lavinia from across the lighted cage, her eyes glittering with anticipation. Lavinia could not look away. She thought, It's nature.

"Ma'am," the boy said to Lavinia, "would you mind opening that hatch there?"

Lavinia paused on the trailer steps, willing herself not to be sick, one hand against the wall for balance, dizzy with nausea and the slow dawning of something awful—could it be?—one hand pressed to her stomach, knowing now what was there. Certain of it. She tried to make some quick calculations in her head, but she was too irregular, it was hard to remember for sure. No, she thought, no, not possible. We were careful. But it was possible, of course it was. Why hadn't she thought of it before? She sat down on the metal steps with her purse on her lap, drank her Coke in huge gulps, wishing she had another.

"Lavinia?"

Ray walked toward her out of the shadows. "Okay?" he asked, stopping in front of her.

"Yeah." She nodded. "I think so. I don't know." But she was fine, of course she was. She had to be. It could be a lot worse. Couldn't it? She could be dying.

He sat down next to her on the steps and lit a cigarette.

"Guess you know the wife's up in Battleford," he said after a few moments. "At the hospital there."

"Yeah," she said, not really listening, "yeah, Jack said." But she felt like saying, *Listen, I don't care. I don't care about your wife. I don't. I have bigger problems.*

"It's a hell of a thing," he went on. He shrugged. "What was I supposed to do? I can't watch her all the time."

Lavinia looked at him then. "What do you mean? Why would you need to?"

"Oh," he said, taking a long drag on his cigarette, "she'd wander off. Evening, usually. Or at night. I was afraid she'd get hurt. That something would happen. She'd be barefoot sometimes. In her nightgown."

Lavinia shook her head. "To where? Where would she go?"

He shrugged again. "Around. Toward the hills mostly." He paused and flicked his cigarette out into the night. "She made it clear to the lake that last time. Not that she ever knew where she was."

Lake? she wondered, and thought of the pictures that had plastered her bedroom. What lake? One of mine? Redberry? Ministikwan? Buffalo Pound? But before she could ask, Ray said, "When Jack found her."

"Jack?" She was about to add, "My Jack?" but realized how stupid it would sound.

"He took her back, that last time," Ray said. "I couldn't. It was better that way anyhow. She preferred it."

"Jack took her?" Lavinia asked, thinking Ray must be mistaken, thinking she wasn't hearing right, that she was confused. It was too much, all this at once. It didn't make sense. Besides, she and Jack would have been seeing each other by then, engaged maybe; he would have said something. She shook her head. "Were they friends or something?"

"Yeah," Ray said after a minute. "They were friends."

Lavinia felt another rush of nausea, took a deep breath to quell it. They were friends? Jack and—what did he call her? A schizo? She lifted her Coke bottle, forgetting it was empty. She was so thirsty. She looked around for a drinking fountain. A spigot. A hose, anything. Her stomach was lurching. Her tongue swollen. She didn't need to hear this right now. Didn't need to hear about Ray's wife. She needed to sort out her thoughts. She wished Ray would leave. If he wouldn't, she would have to. Or she would have to tell him, *Please, I need a minute. I need to be alone here.*

Just then she saw Jack, standing beneath the Ferris wheel, awkward in that weird, coloured night air, turning a slow circle as if looking for them. For her. She rose, steadying herself against the trailer.

"Where you going?" Ray asked.

But she didn't answer.

A Hard Witching

Every night last month, Mr. Crosie had come to Edna in what must have been dreams, his hair smoothed back unnaturally from his temples, the dull wool of his good blue suit brightly silvered in the moonlight. *Alf?* she would say softly, though she would be thinking *Mr. Crosie*, just as she had done all through their married life. *Alf?* But Mr. Crosie would just stand there in the space between the tall bureau and the window, his long arms dangling loose at his sides, palms turned strangely away from her. And each time he came, she thought with a certain wonder, How clean his hands are, right down to the fingernails. And she would try hard to think back: Had they been that way for the funeral? And thinking of that, thinking they might not have been, she felt guilty, as if some urgent and possibly distasteful task had been left undone. *What is it, Alf?* she would ask, edging herself up against the pillows and tugging the blanket higher over her chest, her breath pluming out in the air from the open window at Mr. Crosie's elbow. *What is it?*

It happened that way each night for nearly the entire month

of October, while the fields lay fallow and newly damp with frost and the leaves of the shelter belt slowly yellowed and thinned, and the hens in the yard chortled and shivered and plumped their fat white bodies against the growing cold. But then, the last Saturday of the month, Mr. Crosie did not come. Edna woke late in the morning with the sun already laid out heavily across the bed and, realizing he had not come, dropped to her knees and said out loud, half-relieved, half-alarmed, "Oh, Lord, oh, Lord, do not let the flood sweep over me, Lord, or the deep swallow me up, or the pit close its mouth over me." She did not know why she said it, only that it felt like a thing that should be said. And feeling somehow better for having said it—and being a practical woman, a point upon which she took pride—she rose and fried herself a breakfast of eggs and sausages, which she ate in huge heavily peppered bites straight from the pan, slick with grease and still smoking.

In fact, Edna felt so much better that, for the first time in months, she did not really think anymore of Mr. Crosie. Instead, with a fierce energy she had not known in years, she threw open all the windows to the sharp, good air and began her fall cleaning, pulling down curtains and shaking out rugs to the sunlight with a snap of her wrist; rubbing walls, ceilings and floors briskly with water so hot her hands came away a raw, bright red. And she did not think of Mr. Crosie. She worked that way late into the evening, pegging up the last load of linens on the clothesline under a harvest moon with coyotes yapping their soulless yap from somewhere far beyond the circle of yard light and new frost faintly scenting the air, and she did not think of Mr. Crosie and she did not rest until she collapsed finally in an aching and satisfied heap beside the orange cat on the chesterfield and slept deeply under an afghan she had knitted herself shortly after her marriage; slept smelling the fine lemon smell of a clean house. And she did

not think of Mr. Crosie—not until early the following morning, Sunday, when, just as the last batch of butter tarts for the
church bake sale was browning nicely in her oven, the well
went inexplicably dry. She did not know at first that the well
had gone dry, assumed that it was some small thing wrong
with the pipes that caused the kitchen faucet to choke and
shudder and spit furiously.

"Isn't that just the way," she said to herself rather good-
naturedly, "and Mr. Crosie gone not eight months."

But when she checked the rest of the faucets in the house—
first remembering to remove the tarts from the oven—and
then the outside taps, only to find they all rasped dryly, she
realized she might have a bigger problem on her hands. She
frowned and propped her fists on her hips, surveying the farmyard through narrowed eyes, as if she might spot new misfortunes lurking among the neat red and white granaries.

"It doesn't rain," she said aloud, "but it pours."

Much to Edna's dismay, Heddy Kretsch said a similar thing
that afternoon in the church basement as she watched Edna
arrange butter tarts on a large paper doily the unseasonal
shape of a snowflake. Edna was embarrassed about the doily
and annoyed that Heddy, of all people, had seen it. But Heddy
paid it no attention, interested as she was in the knowledge that
Edna's well had gone dry.

"There's one thing you can count on sure," Heddy said.
"Trouble comes in threes." And then, as if to confirm the fact,
she lifted two spidery fingers in the shape of a V. "That's two."

Edna bit her lip. It would take Heddy to say something like
that. Likely as not, she was drunk. No wonder most people
wouldn't give her the time of day. Just goes to show, Edna

thought, just goes to show. She pointedly edged the Tupperware container of tarts away from Heddy, who, fingering them
as she spoke, turned them slowly, like dials. It was a well-known
fact that Heddy's hands were never what you'd call clean.

"You better watch out," Heddy said. "You got one more
coming."

"Oh, baloney," Edna said. "Silliness. And superstition. I've
got no truck with that nonsense." Nor for you either, she
wanted to add, but instead said, "No good Christian should."
This was a direct jab at the Kretsches, always the first to arrive
and the last to leave, be it church or bar. She snapped the lid
back on the Tupperware container and waved tightly to Leona
Hilling two tables down, hoping she might take the hint and
step over for a chat. She did not.

"I don't know," Heddy said. "Your well gone dry"—she
shook her head slowly, sorrowfully—"and the grass not even
grown over Alf's grave."

Edna flinched at the sound of Mr. Crosie's name on those
lips. She set her jaw and fixed her eyes firmly on a jumble of
canvas banners rolled up and leaning against each other in the
far corner. One had unravelled a bit and Edna could read, in
faded purple lettering, *hine is the kingdo*.

"Edna," Heddy said sharply, rapping her knuckles three
times against the table, "what you got is no ordinary well run
dry. What you got," she said, "is a haint."

Edna, who at first thought Heddy'd said *hate*, stood there
slightly surprised and disturbed at the word.

"I don't *hate*," she began distinctly.

"*Haint*," Heddy stressed, taking pains to enunciate each letter, "you got a *haint*. And he drunk up all your water. Ghosts
are thirsty—"

"Ghosts!" Edna could not think of anything to add. She was
certain now: Heddy was drunk.

"Water's the first thing they look for," Heddy went on reasonably. "You get you some buckets of water and set them all around your bed in a kind of horseshoe shape."

Edna shivered. Mr. Crosie standing silent in his funeral clothes each night by the cold blue light of the moon. Stupid, she thought then, don't be stupid, Edna, you were dreaming. In a dream, she thought, anything is possible.

"Rod's sister in Val Marie," Heddy was saying. "She give her husband a real nice funeral and didn't wear nothing but black and went to the cemetery every day to sit by his grave and cry like there was no tomorrow—more fool her because I known him all my life just about and he was worth maybe three tears at best. But she done everything she could so Marv, that's her husband, didn't have nothing to complain about, so to speak. But then she started finding her geese dead, necks broke, just laid out in the yard every morning. There wasn't no blood, so she knew it wasn't dogs or coyotes or skunks or nothing. It was a haint for sure. So she up and put out buckets of water like I said and goose feathers around her bed and sprinkled pepper around all the doors and windows—"

"Stop it," Edna said.

"Your haint found its own water," Heddy went on.

"Speak like a Christian, for heaven's sake," Edna snapped. "You're in a church."

They stared at each other across the table. Then Heddy pursed her lips, as if considering something.

"If you believe in God," she said flatly, "you believe in ghosts."

For a moment, Edna could not think of a reply, and so she just stood there, feeling the slow, hot beat of her pulse in her temples until Heddy shrugged and plucked a pastry crumb from the edge of the table, rolling it between her fingertips. "All I'm saying is it's better to be prepared. Call it what you want." Then she leaned in so close, Edna could feel sour breath against her face. "Acts of God," she whispered. And popping the crumb in her mouth, she walked away, her thin legs moving sharp and precise as the blades of scissors.

Edna fumed. Heddy—how dare she. Her and that whole pack of dirty, drunken Kretsches and their scrawny, ragged, thieving kids and never a penny to their names—yes, they should be the ones to talk about God. Shouldn't they just. Then, watching Heddy poke her way alone and ignored from table to table, hands jammed deep in the pockets of her dirty brown coat, not buying anything (of course not, how could she?), Edna relented a little. Judge not, lest ye be judged, she thought. There was a lot of truth in that. It was something Mr. Crosie had always said, and she'd almost always given her wholehearted assent. *Yes, indeed, you said it, Mr. Crosie, that's for sure. Judge not.* It was a good motto to live by. Also, There but for the grace of God go I. That was a good one, too.

Edna watched Heddy slip something from the crafts table into the pocket of her coat, something glittery and round, a Christmas ornament perhaps. For a moment, Edna was delighted with the grace of the motion, with the way the silvery object had flashed briefly, then disappeared into that dark pocket like a falling star. But as soon as she'd thought it, the beauty was gone. Isn't that just the way, she thought then. The minute you're inclined to think charitably of someone, they go and do a thing like that. There but for the grace of God, indeed. How about, You reap what you sow? You reap what you sow (even Mr. Crosie would have agreed with her there), be it in this life or the next. And where would they be—people like the Kretsches—on that final day? Not burned up in hell-fire, Edna didn't believe in that holy roller business—she was a Catholic, after all—but maybe just waiting, hands raised to the heavens for a mercy that would never come. Not even realizing they'd been missed. No, not missed, she corrected herself, passed over. That was the sad thing. Well, she sighed, it would all come out in the wash. She didn't know why Heddy irritated her so much. Ghosts. No, what had she called them? Haints. What nonsense, and then she laughed a little. If Heddy Kretsch can get my goat, she thought, I'm a sorry case indeed.

The following morning, Edna phoned around about bringing someone out to the farm to drill a new well. The estimates they gave her were nothing short of shocking. And there was no guarantee, they said, they couldn't make any promises. What did they mean by that? she asked them. They said, Chances are you got water out there somewhere, but how much drilling we do to find it, that's another story. We'll drill as many holes as it takes, they said, but we charge by the foot. I'll have to think about it, she told them. You do that, the last fellow agreed, but don't think too long. Once that ground's froze, you won't get anyone out there. Buggers up the drill bits.

So Edna thought about it. She thought about it as she loaded the half-ton with clean five-gallon pails, she thought about it as she drove the few miles over to Thaubergs' to stock up on water, she thought about it as she filled the buckets from the hose by the barn and then, as he loaded them back into the truck for her, she asked Eulan Thauberg what he thought.

"Oh," he said, heaving a pail up on the bed and sliding it back against the cab in one motion, "I don't know, Edna. Seems like a shame, all this at once."

"If you're going to tell me trouble comes in threes . . ." Edna said, rather sharply. She needed no one's pity, certainly not Eulan Thauberg's. Truth be known, Mr. Crosie might have had many more good winters in him if he hadn't run himself ragged after Eulan Thauberg. *Eulan needs another hand with the seeding* (or the harvesting or the butchering or Lord knows what all else), Mr. Crosie would say and off he'd go, never mind Thaubergs had two sons nearly grown. Never mind his own work at home, always a dollar short and a day late.

Eulan Thauberg frowned. "No," he said, "I wasn't thinking that." He scratched his chin, heaved up another pail. "Just that," he said, leaning over the side of the truck, "it's a long winter out here, you know?"

Edna did know. Of course she did, she'd lived around these parts her entire life. Eulan knew that. What was he getting at?

"It's just," Eulan went on, hoisting up the last pail with a puff, "maybe you might think about moving to town now."

"Town! Eulan, how can you even think it!" But she knew exactly how Eulan could think it; he had his eye on her land. That was like him. She was surprised he'd waited this long. "No," Edna said firmly, "I won't leave the place. I just need the well fixed up and I'll be all set." She considered. "How many holes will they have to drill, do you think?"

Eulan slammed the tailgate shut and leaned against it.

"Oh, they're pretty good usually," he said. "They hit the low spots first. You got a good one west of the barn there. Around here, they have to go down fifteen, twenty-five feet or so."

Edna calculated the estimate they'd given her per foot. "If they have to drill more than once, that could get pretty costly," she said, mostly to herself. And then, for some reason, a memory came upon her, of that hole she and Mr. Crosie had found beside the road allowance, out past the Sand Hills—when was it? Years ago. *Pull over*, he'd said suddenly as they bumped along. *What for?* she'd wanted to know. *Just pull over*, he said. So she did, and he unfolded his body from the cab of the truck and walked back along the road. She waited a while. Then, when she saw he was making no move to return, she followed him.

He was standing at the side of the road, holding an old cream can lid, rusted and dented almost beyond recognition. There was a hole cut in the middle, roughly the size of a quart sealer or a little bigger. Mr. Crosie turned the lid slowly in his large hands. *What in the world*, Edna said, *have you got that for?* Mr. Crosie nudged the ground with the toe of his boot. *It was over this hole here.* Edna looked down. There was a hole in the ground, about the size of the hole in the lid. Mr. Crosie picked up a stone and dropped it down. Edna counted to herself. It was fifteen, no, almost twenty seconds before they heard it hit bottom. They blinked at each other. Mr. Crosie shook his head in disbelief, dropped another stone, and they waited again until it hit. Dry. *By the size of it, looks like an old test hole. For a well*, Mr. Crosie said, amazement in his voice. Then he shook his head again. *What's so strange about that?* Edna asked. Mr. Crosie lifted his hands, looked around. *There's not a farm around here for three, four miles at least*, he said, *never has been that I know of. This is community pasture.* Edna took the cream can lid. *This has been here a while*, she said. She ran her thumb around the rim, rusted to a thin, lacy edge. Mr. Crosie nodded. *Rusted right into the ground there. Had to pry it up.* He took his lighter from his pants pocket—the good silver-plated lighter she'd given him for Christmas a few years back, engraved with his initials—and bent over the hole, trying, quite foolishly Edna thought, to see by that small blue light. *If you drop that*, Edna warned, *I can tell you you'll be coming back here tonight with a shovel.* After a moment, Mr. Crosie straightened and pocketed the lighter. He looked around again, removed his cap. *I can't figure it out*, he said. Edna tossed the lid down; it landed partway over the hole with a soft *plunk*. *Oh well*, she said, *we aren't going to solve this mystery.* And she started back for the truck. *Come on*, she hollered over her shoulder, *I've got supper on.* She stopped and looked back in time to see Mr. Crosie straighten the lid so it fit neatly over the hole, then step it gently into place.

He'd talked about that hole for weeks after, months. He'd pipe up suddenly, while thumbing through *The Producer* or in the middle of *M*A*S*H*, *Who could have drilled it? Someone from around here? What for? When?* It always took her a few seconds to clue in. *Who cares?* she'd say then. *Forget about it already.* But he couldn't. In fact, she'd bet dollars to doughnuts he'd been back there with a flashlight more than once. Mr. Crosie was like that, couldn't leave things alone. Silly things. Useless things. It annoyed her.

Edna blinked up into sunlight. Eulan stared at her.

"I said, have you had someone down there even? Might be you just need to dump a load of water in, get someone down to prime the pump. You should get someone down there once before you go and bring the drillers out."

Edna took a long breath. "I hadn't thought of that," she said, exhaling. "You'd think they might've said something about that on the phone."

"What have you got there anyway," Eulan asked, "jet pump or submersible?"

"Submersible?" Edna asked.

"A down-hole submersible," he said, then added, "Is your pump by the house or down the well?"

"Oh," Edna said, "I really don't know." *I should know that*, she thought angrily. *Why don't I know that?*

Eulan shrugged. "Either way, it's worth a try, I guess," he said. "Hell of a lot cheaper than drilling a new well. Betty's brother had to go down sixty-five feet and she was dry as toast. Hell of a lot cheaper than that."

"Yes," Edna said absently, for she was still trying to think whether she'd seen anything like a pump near the house, "that's for sure. You said it."

"Well, then, you just hang on there once," Eulan said, and thumped a fist against the truck. "You just hang on," he said. "I know a fella."

. . .

Edna drove home, the water slopping out on the truck bed with each bump in the road. Just as well, she thought, listening to it slosh and roll behind her. Full pails would be too heavy for her to lift anyway. You'd think Eulan could have figured that out for himself. You'd think, after all Mr. Crosie had done for him, he would have offered to haul some over for her, or at least have one of the boys do it. But that was Eulan. She'd noticed he hadn't offered to check the pump for her either. Well, that was no real surprise; she'd known Eulan Thauberg too long to expect it of him. No, he had his eye on the land, all right. But he had another thing coming. Typical Eulan: greedy. Greedy and cheap. Lazy, too.

But this fellow Eulan mentioned sounded promising; a young fellow from near Golden Prairie—she didn't recognize the name. She hoped he worked fast. That chill in the air even at midday promised a hard frost. Soon the ground would freeze; it would be too late to drill if she needed to. Besides, she couldn't keep hauling water from Thaubergs', she fretted as she pulled into the quiet yard and unloaded the wet, heavy buckets straight into the porch. It just didn't make sense.

And, thinking about how things did not make sense, Edna pulled off her coat and boots and sat at the kitchen table far into the evening, waiting for the phone to ring, staring out the window as the sun slowly turned a dull, effortless red and sank beneath the horizon. In the dark, she rested her head on her arms and thought that sometimes, sometimes, it was all just too much.

When Edna woke the next morning, the muscles in her neck aching and the orange cat demanding to be let out and the water crusted over in the unheated porch (for she had forgotten to bring any into the house), she began to think Eulan Thauberg was right. Maybe she should leave the farm. She lugged one of the pails into the kitchen and chopped half-heartedly at the surface with the wooden handle of a butcher knife and thought, for some reason, of Heddy Kretsch, her lean, sharp face; she thought about trouble coming in threes. Maybe Heddy, too, was right. She put a kettle on to boil for coffee, then washed her face in the icy water and sat again at the kitchen table. Mr. Crosie, the well. Against all her prior reasoning, she began to suspect a connection between the two.

Then Monson appeared.

"It doesn't rain," Edna said to him, this time forcing a cheerful smile, as he stepped down from his truck, "but it sure does pour." Now that Monson was here, she'd decided it wouldn't do to mope around about things that couldn't be helped. She smoothed her skirt and stepped back a little as he turned a slow circle, surveying the yard.

He was smaller, much smaller than she'd imagined, and even a little younger than Eulan had led her to believe, though it was hard to tell when a man kept his hair. And what hair he had, forking up all over his head in sharp black curls. As if reading her mind, Monson jammed his cap down low over his flat, rather pointed ears and stared at her from beneath the brim with bright, dark eyes. Edna peered back. She didn't really like the looks of him. There was something gnomelike, something shifty, unclean. As though all his edges were blurred. He looked like a drinker. Finally, she thrust her hand forward and said, a little uneasily, "I'm Mrs. Crosie."

"Monson." He grinned, rather unexpectedly revealing a row of teeth, white and even and delicate as pearls. Edna wondered if they could be real.

"Eulan said he thought you had a submersible," he said, "but that you weren't sure."

Submersible, Edna thought, there's that word again. "I believe it is a submersible, Mr. Monson," she said with authority. "There's certainly no jet pump that I can see." She said *jet pump* distinctly.

Monson gave her an odd look. "Okay," he said, "I guess I'll check the well then."

"I'll walk you over." She wanted to ask how long all this might take. There had been flurries in the air yesterday, sailing past the kitchen window, though today it was slightly warmer, the sun beaming down on the yard as if heaven itself was sending her hope and goodwill.

"There it is," Edna said, pointing to the three-foot-high wellhouse.

Monson walked over, unlatched the heavy wooden lid and peered inside with an enormous flashlight he'd unhooked from his belt.

"You got oak casings here," he said, tapping the flashlight against the inside of the well. "Original, looks like."

"Oh?" Edna followed him over, unsure what it meant to have oak casings. Surely not good, not if they were original. Would they need to be replaced, too?

"Don't see that much anymore," Monson said, leaning back and clicking off the flashlight. "This must be the genuine article."

Edna blinked. "You mean the original well?"

"Must be. Don't find oak casings these days." He laughed. "Not a lot of oak trees around here."

Edna nodded. She didn't really like the fellow's laugh.

Monson hooked the flashlight back on his belt the way Mr. Crosie used to knock the ashes from his cigarette without tapping it against anything, holding it backhand between his thumb and pointer fingers, flicking it with his index. A quick, smooth motion as natural as breathing. One of the things she'd first noticed about Mr. Crosie. Funny to remember that still, thirty, no, nearly forty years later.

Monson patted the wellhouse. "She's dry," he said, "that's for sure."

Well, I already knew that, Edna thought.

"I'll go down and check the pump."

Edna peeked over the side of the well. "How will you get down?"

But Monson was already uncoiling a long, thick length of rope, the kind Mr. Crosie had used for bridles back when he'd still kept horses, before she'd finally convinced him they weren't worth the cost of feed. Pets, they were; useless. The cat, now, at least it was good for something.

"It's wide enough," Monson said, "so I don't have to go down headfirst. I can climb back out."

"Headfirst!" Edna said. "Surely not."

"Usually not enough room for a man to turn around." He glanced at her with another of those brilliant smiles. "Even a man my size."

Edna blushed, looked away. Could he read her mind?

"If you don't go down headfirst . . ." he said, and shrugged.

Edna tried to imagine being lowered down a well headfirst, into the earth, like a worm. She shivered and rubbed her arms.

Monson tied a fat knot to the outside of the wellhouse, tested it by throwing all his weight into it, then clipped the end of the rope to a kind of leather harness he wore around his hips. As he climbed over the edge, Edna barely suppressed an urge to

shout, *Don't!* Instead she asked nervously, "Won't you just drop
. . . straight down?" She eyed the loose coil of rope on the
ground. "It's all slack."

Monson grinned. "Just watch."

So Edna watched as he braced his compact shoulders and
back against one side of the well, his feet firmly against the
other, and began to edge himself slowly down, feet then shoulders, feet then shoulders. It looked so effortless. Still, she was
uneasy. She didn't relish the thought of a dead man tied to a
rope at the bottom of her well.

"You got a good wide one here," Monson said as his black
curls disappeared into the well. "Hand-dug most likely, considering that casing."

There was a sound of earth falling, and Edna pressed her
hands to her mouth.

"It's okay," Monson called up, though his voice had a
strange, ghostly echo now. "Just dirt behind the casings."

Edna peered over the edge. Even with the sunlight beaming
down into the mouth of the well, she could not see Monson,
just a shadow, the suggestion of something moving. And the
shh-shh sound as he edged his way deeper. Soon even that
stopped. Edna waited, feeling her skin crawl. It disturbed her
that she could no longer see him.

"All right down there?" she called, knowing her palms had
begun to sweat.

"All right," he called. And then the flashlight clicked on and
Edna could see all the way to the bottom. Oh, she thought,
that's not so deep. She leaned over the side and breathed the
cold smell of earth, like root cellars, like digging potatoes.

Below, Monson moved in the yellow light, twisting around
and clanging something against the metal pump. She could see
his boots sticking and sucking against the muddy bottom. It
was a strange sensation, looking down on him that way, his

small shadow moving over and across the light, as though she had captured some elf and held him in a pit for safekeeping. *Peter, Peter, pumpkin-eater*, she thought, and laughed to herself, even though she knew the rhyme didn't really make sense. Still, there was something funny about it. *Had a wife and couldn't keep her, put her in a dried-up well . . .*

Monson looked up then, his face lit from below, yellow and awful, seeming to leer at her with undisguised malice. Edna stepped quickly back, repressed an impulse to slam the lid shut and run.

"Your pump's done for," he hollered up.

What's the matter with me, Edna thought, trying to breathe evenly, slowly, to calm her thumping heart. I'm so nervous these days. Stupid, she thought, don't be stupid. She approached the well again, but did not look down.

"What's wrong with it?" she called.

"Nothing," he yelled, "everything. It's just done for. Old. Worn out."

Edna heard the *click* of the flashlight being turned off, saw the rope move against the lip of the well, like something crawling in. She peeked over the side but could see nothing. Staring into the darkness, she breathed in the good earth smell and listened to the thump-*shh* sound of him climbing up, a different sound from when he went down. As her eyes adjusted to the darkness and the man grew nearer, she could make out his shape coming slowly toward her, and she was overcome by an awful terror, as if everything evil in the world was about to climb up out of that pit. Slam the lid, she thought, slam it quick and lock it. There's still time. But then Monson's face hit the light and she saw that he was, after all, only a man.

• • •

"She's pretty much run dry," Monson said, as they walked up the rise back to the house. He carried the old pump. "You can try and get this fixed," he said, "but it looks done to me."

"But there was mud," Edna said. "I saw it."

Monson shrugged. "Couple days that'll be gone, too. Trouble is, she's not filling back up. Wells are ground-fed. She should have filled back up some by now."

"So I'll have to drill then," Edna said, not quite believing him. If there was water before, why should the well run dry all of a sudden? Why now? She wondered if she shouldn't get a second opinion.

Monson spat. "Looks like."

They stood near the porch, staring back down at the old wellhouse.

"Look on the bright side," he said. "At least you can get it drilled. At least you don't have to do it by hand. With shovels."

Edna did not, at that moment, wish to look on the bright side. She fixed her gaze on the treasonous wellhouse, its metal sides glinting with infuriating cheer in the sun. Funny—she didn't think she'd ever noticed before today that it was metal.

"They used to be wood," Monson said.

Edna started. She did not turn to look at him as he continued.

"Prairie fires'd come through in the summer, burn 'em to the ground. Men would come back exhausted at night after fighting a fire all day, maybe longer." He spat again. "It was dark. They couldn't see."

Edna shivered. What a terrible thing to say. Why would he say that?

"That's why they're metal now."

She looked at him, standing not two feet from her, the heavy iron pump in his hand, and she thought, He could strike me down with that right now, it would take just one blow . . .

"Thank you for your time, Mr. Monson," she said quickly. "What do I owe you?"

He squinted for a moment out at the horizon. Edna waited. She wasn't really afraid, she knew that. It was the strain. She was tired.

"You gonna drill a new well?" he asked.

Now what? she thought. "I guess I have to."

He worked his mouth, as if he were about to spit again, but he didn't. "I can witch it for you," he said finally, "if you want."

Edna shook her head, was about to say, Certainly not, Mr. Monson, I don't believe in that nonsense. Instead she stopped, considered the cost of digging more than one hole. Witching. What could it hurt?

"How much?" she asked.

Monson speculated. "Oh, let's say fifty, for everything."

Edna pursed her lips. That sounded pretty steep. Of course, she thought, I'm a widow. It wouldn't surprise her if this fellow were in cahoots with Eulan Thauberg. She'd have to keep her eye on him, that was for sure.

"All right," she said. "Go ahead."

They turned to walk back to the house.

"Might take a while," he said, "what with the cold."

"What's that got to do with it? Surely the ground's not frozen yet." She stopped to chop at the earth with the heel of her boot. Monson looked at her as though she were simple-minded.

"Not the ground," he said, "currents."

Currents were frozen? What currents? She watched suspiciously as he walked to his truck and lifted something out through the open window.

"Energy currents," he said over his shoulder.

"Mr. Monson," she began firmly, but then she saw that he held an old box, brown and peeling, tied shut with a fraying loop of cord. He noticed her stare.

"Tools of the trade," he said, giving the box a pat and tucking it up under his arm.

"I hope you know," Edna said, resuming her firm tone, "I don't ordinarily take up with this nonsense."

Monson shrugged. "Desperate measures," he said. And he grinned.

So he did think she was desperate, Edna mused with a considerable degree of dissatisfaction, watching from the kitchen window as Monson paced the yard, still carrying that box tucked up under one arm. From this distance, he looked like a child, a boy, scuffing his boots through the dirt. She wondered what she'd seen threatening in him. Edna glanced at the clock over the stove. He'd been stalking around the yard for the better part of an hour. When would he get to business? She had to admit she was curious. She wondered what Mr. Crosie would think. Probably that it was a fine idea. She sighed and shook her head. That had always been the difference between the two of them. Even back before they'd married, Edna could see that Mr. Crosie was gullible, easily taken in. His naïveté had appealed to her then, in a way. But it soon became tiresome. She'd told him as much on several occasions, as recently as that past spring, just weeks before he died. Mr. Crosie had come in late again from helping Eulan seed.

"People take advantage," she'd called out to the porch when she heard him come in. She set a plate of ham and boiled potatoes she'd been keeping warm sharply down on the table and poured a cup of coffee. "You believe any sob story going around. But you wait and see if any of them are there when you need a hand. You wait and see."

She had peeked around the corner. Mr. Crosie was seated on the darkened stairs leading up from the porch, pulling off a boot in one long, tired motion. He had his back to her, and Edna thought for a moment that he could have been his own father, gone but five years that winter. He looked that old, that hunched, his thin shadow curled on the wall behind him. And for a moment, Edna felt inexplicably sad. She had been about to say, *You're no spring chicken*, a phrase that always made Mr. Crosie cluck and flap his arms, high-stepping his lanky body in an absurd parody—an action that, against her will, always made her laugh. She'd been about to say it and then caught herself, aware all at once of the evidence of his age written on every bone, every hard curve of his body. Aware that he felt it, too. And for a moment, for the first time in years, she'd wanted to drop right down on her knees and hold him tightly, so tightly he would say, "Easy now, you'll squeeze the life clean out of me," just as he used to, and she would know—they'd both know—it was only a joke.

But then, as quickly as it had come, the feeling had gone. What good did all that silly mooning about do anyway? she had wondered. She spooned creamed corn on his plate, shook salt and pepper liberally over everything and sat down, waiting for him to join her. It seemed to take him a long time to remove his other boot. "You don't give them enough credit," he said at last, coming stiffly to the table.

"Aren't you going to wash up?" she demanded as he pulled his chair out.

Mr. Crosie looked slowly down at his hands and forearms, grey and powdery with dust caught between the coarse hairs, looked at them as if he'd never seen them before. "Yes," he said, turning his big palms to the light. "Yes, I guess I forgot."

"I guess you did," Edna said as Mr. Crosie headed for the bathroom. "You see how tired you get, all this extra work?" And then, "Who?" she called, as if just remembering. "Don't give who enough credit?"

"Anybody," he'd said, and closed the door behind him.

It wasn't so long ago, but it felt like years. Mr. Crosie'd say things like that to her now and then, odd things. Things Edna felt weren't entirely justified. She was the first to give credit. Where credit was due.

And now there was Monson, stooped down over the box that he'd set on the ground. He untied the cord and opened the lid. Edna craned her neck to see, but Monson had his back to her, blocking her view. In a moment, he rose and turned toward the house. Edna stepped away from the window.

"Mrs. Crosie," he called shortly.

Edna thought, How rude, can't even come to the door. She opened the window a few inches.

"I'll try that low spot west of the barn," he said, "and over by the shelter belt."

Well, she thought, what are you waiting for? But she said, "Fine, fine, go right ahead."

"Can't make any promises," he said.

No, of course you can't, she thought grimly, closing the window. Now, if Mr. Crosie were here, he'd be out there at Monson's heels, toting that box for him, asking all kinds of silly questions, fascinated by what he would think was some sort of magical gift, a gift from God. Monson himself had said currents. There was no magic in that, just science pure and simple. Or so Monson thought. Edna knew better. It wasn't God and it wasn't science. It wasn't anything. She should know. She'd often thought she would have made a good scientist, if she'd had the opportunity. She had that kind of a mind. Not Mr. Crosie, though. Maybe, she thought, chuckling to herself, Mr. Crosie had sent Monson her way, just to rile her up. That would be like him, thinking he was having one over on her. Testing her. Seeing if she could be spooked with all this witching business, all this talk of ghosts. She chuckled again and poured herself a fresh cup of coffee.

Yes, indeed, she thought, watching Monson cross the yard and disappear behind the shelter belt, that's a fine joke. That's a good one.

When Monson had still not reappeared, by noon, Edna told herself, Enough is enough, and pulled on her rubber boots and the old jacket she used for doing chores. For all she knew, he could be having a nap back there. Or worse. Heaven only knew what he carried around in that box. And he did look like a drinker. Lord, Edna thought, that's all I need. That was one thing about Mr. Crosie, he was never a drinker. And she was thankful for it every day of their married life. No, he was never a drinker and he never kept things from her. He'd always said, "Edna, I couldn't keep a thing from you if I tried." Edna always felt a certain satisfaction listening to other women complain about their husbands in that way. She would just sit back and listen and at the right moment say, "Mine, I can read him like an open book." And she could, too. Problem was, Mr. Crosie was never really all that interesting; it was like reading the same page over and over.

This Monson, now, she thought, zipping her jacket and stepping outside, this Monson was another story. He was cut from a different cloth. Oh, he was easy enough to read in one way, that was clear. He was an opportunist. But he was also the kind you needed to keep your eye on, liable to shift at any second. Edna bent to pet the orange cat that wound itself between her ankles. Yes, she decided, he was a slippery one. Straightening, she noticed the sky had lost the wide open blue of that morning, had greyed over in one long sheet. The bland look of a snow sky. The temperature, too, had dropped. She turned up her collar and headed for the shelter belt, the orange cat darting ahead of her, tail twitching.

"Mr. Monson," Edna called, not too loudly, as she neared the trees. Her boots cracked across dead branches. "Mr. Monson?" she repeated, poking through to the other side. But he was nowhere to be seen. The yard stretched out into the edge of the nearby stubble field. Everything had that odd flatness that came with a snow sky, like a picture. All depth sucked out.

"Hello?" she called softly. But the air settled around her as still as the landscape. She puffed out a long cloud of breath and turned south along the shelter belt. Maybe Monson had gone around back already, by the barn.

Edna had almost reached the far end of the yard when she noticed the box. She nearly missed it, really, settled as it was there in the trees, the same dull brown as the dirt and leaves, the cord coiled loosely on top of the lid. She stepped toward it across a rotting stump. "Mr. Monson?" she said again. The orange cat minced along ahead of her, sniffing at the edge of the box, then bounding away into the trees as Edna moved closer, hands stuffed into the pockets of her coat. She stopped and looked slowly up and down the shelter belt. There was no sign of Monson anywhere. Maybe I should just take this along with me, Edna thought. He might be needing it wherever he's got to. Save him the trip back. She looked down the narrow row of trees once more, then bent forward and pushed the cord to one side. The initials A.M. had been carved roughly into the lid. It looked like a homemade job, she thought, probably did it himself. She poked the box with her boot. Really, it wouldn't hurt to have a quick peek. It was on her property, after all, and if there was something inside she should know about, something that shouldn't be there . . . Edna had not really formed any clear notion of what that something might be, only that she wouldn't abide any ill doings on her property. And with that certainty in mind, she lifted the cord and opened the lid.

She stood a moment, breathing the cold afternoon air, the cord dangling loosely from her fingertips.

"Why," she said finally, "it's empty."

She blinked her eyes a couple of times, just to make sure. Then she straightened, her lips pressed firmly together. Empty. Yes, of course it was. The man was no fool, wouldn't leave anything lying around. The place she should have looked was his truck. And she'd had the perfect opportunity, too.

Then, just as she let the lid fall shut and was replacing the cord, Monson appeared through the trees. Before he could speak, she said, "I was just thinking I'd bring you your box." She guessed that he thought he was pretty clever, leaving it sitting there in the open for her to find, to throw her off her guard.

She stared him straight in the face. He looked smaller in the trees, as if the very air was slowly shrinking him. He lifted his hands then, and Edna saw he held a long metal rod in each one. She sucked in her breath and stepped quickly back.

"Brazing rods," he said, "get pretty cold on the hands. Might have to switch to willow."

"Willow?" Edna puffed, eager to hide her momentary start at the appearance of the rods. Now that she saw them clearly, they weren't threatening at all, rather fine and delicate, like kitchen utensils. Almost pretty, really.

"Willow's more accurate anyway," he said, opening the box and laying the rods gently inside, "in cold weather."

Edna stepped forward, "You mean you haven't found water yet?"

Monson closed the lid and tied it shut with the cord. "Might take a while. Like I said." He leaned back on his haunches and looked up at her. Edna was reminded, briefly, of those garden gnomes Mr. Crosie had been fond of.

"Mr. Monson," she said, "you can see for yourself this ground's going to freeze solid any minute now."

"What difference does that make?"

"As I'm sure you know," she snapped, "once the ground freezes, you can't drill."

Monson scowled. "Who told you that?"

Edna could not remember. Had it been Eulan?

"Makes no difference," Monson went on. "They use the same drills to dig oil and gas wells. Up north. In Alaska. Around here, ground freezes maybe six feet, that on a bad year. You can wait till January if you want."

Edna felt the blood rush to her temples as Monson spoke. How dare he lie to her that way? Did he think she was stupid? He was a liar, that's all. A liar and a drinker.

"You think," she began, "you can come out here and have one over on me. Because I'm a widow. A farm widow." Here she paused, as if the significance of this had only just sunk in. And in that second, everything changed. "If Mr. Crosie were here," she said, "if Mr. Crosie were here . . ."

But she didn't know how to finish, and for some reason that she did not understand, tears sprang hotly to her eyes. Mortified, she turned slightly away, looking upward at that grey sheet of sky to keep the tears, oh hateful, from edging down her face. Of all the ridiculous things, she thought, both angry and surprised at herself. And what would this Monson think now?

After a moment, she heard him say quietly, "I'm sorry. Alf Crosie was a good man."

"I beg your pardon?" she said without turning around. "Did you say you knew my husband?"

"Why, sure," he said, sounding surprised.

Of all the lowdown, disgusting things, Edna thought. To lie about this, to pretend he'd ever known Mr. Crosie.

"How?" she demanded, turning slowly to face him. "How did you know him? From where? Tell me."

"I've known Alf for years," he said, "since . . . I guess since that summer he took me and Eulan over to check out an old test well site, out at the Sand Hills there. That's the first time I met him, anyways. Through Eulan."

Edna blinked.

"Alf had a notion there might be more to it. That hole, I mean. Exactly what, he wouldn't ever say. Geez, that was years ago."

But Edna was no longer looking at him. She'd turned away again when she felt the tears come.

"I'm sorry," Monson said quietly behind her. "I'll just go hunt down some willow." And he turned and headed back up the shelter belt, toward the house.

When he disappeared through the trees, Edna wiped her eyes and let out an enormous puff of breath. The man was a liar. A liar and a cheat. And a drinker. And Heddy Kretsch had been right after all. "That's three," she said, "and it won't get the best of me." She'd catch up to him, pay him his money and send him on his way. She imagined what Heddy's reaction would be when she told the story. Oh, trouble comes in threes all right, Edna would say generously, but it's the weak who let it stay. And then she would tell how she'd sent this shyster packing. Good riddance to bad rubbish, she'd say. And she wiped her eyes and congratulated herself again as she looked toward the spot in the trees where Monson had disappeared. And then, thinking of that, thinking of Monson disappearing into the trees, Edna had a terrible thought. She'd left the house unlocked. And everything, her jewellery, her wallet, the new television, oh, it was all there. How could I have been so stupid, she thought as she started to run along the shelter belt, her body heaving against its own weight. How could I have been so stupid? Already she was huffing to catch her breath in the cold. She'd never make it back to the house in time. He'd take it all, he'd take everything, her wedding ring sitting where she always left it by the sink.

Edna ran faster, rubber boots clomping loosely over rocks and twigs. She thought for a moment that she might make it after all, but just as she was nearing the break in the trees, something small and fast darted between her legs. Edna shrieked and stumbled, one boot pulling free as she twisted an ankle across a fallen branch. She hit the ground hard, harder than she thought possible, her hip catching the sharp end of a stone. She lay dazed as the orange cat bounded back toward her, stopping to sniff wetly at her ear. She pushed it away and rolled over, struggling to pull into a sitting position, but she felt a tremendous weight on her chest. And a hard, shooting pain ran from her hip to her ankle. She looked down at her feet, noticing that one of her socks had pulled off with the rubber boot. How white and foolish her foot looked sticking up that way against the dark line of trees. She began to laugh, in short, painful gasps.

Good riddance, Edna thought again as she laid her head back, still puffing to catch her breath. But this time there was no satisfaction in the phrase, no sense of justice. "Good riddance," she said out loud, testing the words on her tongue. They were flimsy, could have been any words at all. She stared up at the sky, now the dull, hard colour of iron, and noticed the snow had started, just barely, the flakes so fine they could have been dust. So fine they could have passed over someone else unnoticed, someone who didn't happen to be looking up. And much to her dismay, Edna felt the tears start again. She opened her eyes wide as the cold, still air settled around her. "What is it, Alf?" she whispered, snowflakes dissolving in the palms of her hands. "What is it?"

The Ghost
of Ingebrigt Lake

The house, of course, is dark. It is the one thing he cannot get used to, even after all these years. Wesley stops the half-ton just inside the caragana shelter and kills the engine. He keeps the lights on a moment, watching rain slice through the beams and disappear. When he'd left the farm that morning, he'd been surprised at the bit of snow, still hard and blue, sloped against the north side of the granaries, as if someone had hidden it there, hopefully, packing it against the lower planks in tight drifts for some long afternoon in August. Everywhere else, the yard was wet with the thaw and the rain that would make seeding tomorrow, the next day, all week maybe, impossible. This rain, he thinks, this damned rain that's so good to come, we need it, but even so it's hateful. There'll be no work now for a while.

He cuts the lights and steps out, planting his feet carefully against the muddy yard. Ahead, the farmhouse seems to tilt at

an absurd angle, a trick of the rain slanting through the yardlight, setting the buildings, the trees, the old windmill frame, at
odds with where he knows the flat line of the horizon would lie.
Driving in sometimes at night, he can't believe this is his home
at all, that he has ever lived here—that anyone has. It seems
unlikely that light has ever shone from those windows, unlikely
the screen door has creaked open and clattered shut a dozen
times a day, more.

It seems impossible.

By the time he reaches the porch, he is soaked through. He
peels off his coat in the entrance and then his shirt, too, and his
socks, stiffly, rubs his neck and chest with an old wool sweater
of his father's from a peg by the door, then pulls it on over his
head. It is short in the sleeves, and he thinks that maybe it
wasn't his father's after all, but his mother's. Was it? For a
moment, he feels that fleeting sense of disorientation, like stepping out into a windless snowfall, watching those flakes and
thinking they are not falling, it is your own body rising,
through them. But the feeling lasts only a moment, and then
the unwelcome surprise of cold in the kitchen rouses him. He
takes a matchbook from the tobacco tin over the stove and
goes barefoot down to the empty cellar. He comes here only
rarely now, to relight the furnace or in summer to store food
that would quickly turn in the close heat of the rooms above.
But once, the walls had been lined with jars, shining neatly by
the light of the bare bulb overhead, pickles and beets and
rhubarb. Sometimes the soft white flesh of trout from the river,
smoked and packed in pint sealers. Jellies, clear amber and
purple. Tomatoes. Could there have been so many? All those
jars, is it possible? He remembers his mother in the kitchen,

dipping from enormous paper bags with the tin measuring cup he still uses, salt for the pickles, sugar for the fruit. He remembers her scrubbing and blanching and straining pulp through a piece of old window screen, her face red with the steam, her lips moving almost soundlessly to a song he never could figure out, though he held his breath to listen. He remembers helping his father to cut the screen, stretching it taut against his own knees, *Hold on tight there, Wes,* winking and setting the blade against the screen. *You don't want to lose a limb now, eh? What would your mother say?* And Wesley gripped the edge of the screen so fiercely, it bit into the palms of his hands.

He remembers that. And he should. He should remember it all. He should remember his mother calling from the porch, *Don't torment the child. You want to give him nightmares?* And his father looking up at him from under his brows. *You won't go and have nightmares on your mother, will you now? If you swear it, I'll tell you a tale that'll curl your nosehairs.* And he'd nodded his head emphatically. *Yes, yes, I promise.* And he meant it. His father's stories were not frightening, not in that way. They would sit at the kitchen table, the three of them round the yellow lamp, his mother mending, his father fiddling with a harness or a broken axle or a watch. And Wesley quiet, hands under his knees, waiting for his father to begin.

Back in the days before the homestead rush, when there was still buffalo to be had and the land was yet unbroken, there came a surveyer named Robert John McCallum, an Englishman, not much to look at, but a hell of a shot from the saddle or the soil. He was here on a survey expedition, like I say, and shacked up with the rest of them fellas at Chesterfield House. But something got to him, the wind maybe, or the sun, the way it can here where a man might mistake his shadow stretching a mile long for his own self, if you know what I mean, and this McCallum just took up one day with his horse and pitched a skin-tent over there by that sorry alkali slough they call Ingebrigt Lake. Couple of the men went by one day, thinking they'd talk some sense into him, bring him on back. But they didn't get within ten yards before they was staring down the barrel of his Winchester. "Come on now, McCallum," they called. "We brought you some food is all." And one of the men patted a haversack he carried slung behind his saddle. But McCallum didn't move a muscle, just stood there pointing that rifle, his hair wild from the wind and his face brown as his boots. "This country knocked the English right out of you," one of the men said, thinking to joke with him. But McCallum stood his ground, stood it so long the men finally turned tail and rid back to Chesterfield House, ready to give him up for a goner. But the Mounties here didn't like to encourage that kind of behaviour, so when they got wind of what McCallum had done, two of them rid over from Montgomery's Landing. They had their pistols ready, aiming to take McCallum by force if necessary. They rid up, and seeing his horse hobbled a few yards off, called, "Robert John McCallum, by order of the Queen we demand you to come out now with your hands up. We don't want trouble. We just want you to come on back. There's savages enough out here without losing one of our own." Then they sat and waited, their horses snorting and stamping in the dust and the wind rattling the walls of that tent, skimming out over the surface of the lake in ridges. They waited, and when McCallum showed neither hide nor hair, they rushed the tent, fearing any minute to take a bullet from behind those skin walls rattling and snapping away in the wind. But it wasn't Robert John McCallum of Worcestershire, England, they found sitting in that skin-tent. No, it wasn't McCallum they found, nor no man, alive or dead. They found nothing but a few empty cans and his Winchester leaned up in the corner. That and McCallum's horse outside. One of the Mounties looked out over the lake. "Is there enough water in that slough to drown a man?" he asked. "Not likely," said the other. "Unless you're trying awful hard." So they took up McCallum's horse, rolled up his tent with the rifle inside, then headed back to the landing. "He'll turn up," they said, "sooner or later." Well, it wasn't long before he did turn up, so to speak. One of W.D. Smith's boys—he used to run his cattle over there—reported seeing a light on the shore of Ingebrigt Lake, like a campfire or something. When he rid over to *check it out, thinking to scare off some half-breeds, the light disappeared. Sort of flickered slowly out the closer he got. When he reached the shore, there was no sign of a recent fire anywhere. Everybody thought he was crazy, of course. Then other folks started seeing it, too. For years, decades. Sometimes it burned red, like fire, sometimes it just kind of glowed, more of a faint blue, like a lantern. Some said it was the ghost of Robert John McCallum out looking for his horse. Maybe it's true. I surely don't know. If it is, he's been looking for that horse a long time.*

If it is, Wesley's father said, leaning close to the yellow light, *I'm awful sorry for the poor soul. He's been looking a mighty long time.*

But here in the cellar is this furnace that won't light. Wesley strikes a third match; the flame catches, burning a small steady blue, and he pulls the length of red yarn attached to the bulb, feeling his way carefully back up the narrow stairs in darkness.

As he reaches the top, he thinks he hears a knock at the screen door. He stops, listens, hears it again. Yes. For a moment, he wonders whether he should pretend he is not home. But he has left the light burning in the kitchen, his truck parked in the yard. He lets the cellar door fall shut, peeks through the kitchen window, through the rain, but can see no vehicle other than his own. And he thinks, Maybe I have imagined it then, made something else of the rain, my own breathing. Maybe owls. They come now sometimes in bad weather.

"Hello?" a voice calls from outside. "Anybody home?"

He does not move to answer right away, afraid that if he opens the door, there will be no one, just the rain and the mud and the yardlight. His truck and the caraganas and beyond them only the night, nothing. He waits, deciding, and the door edges open, a head pokes in.

"Yes?" Wesley says, lurching forward. "What is it?"

He can see by the way the boy falls back into the rain that Wesley has scared him.

"We got—" the boy says. "Sorry to bother you—"

"What is it?" He does not want to frighten the boy. He flicks on the porch light and the boy flinches. He is young, a teenager; water runs in a stream from the peak of his cap.

"I got stuck," he says, wiping the back of his hand across his nose, "out towards the Sand Hills." He jerks vaguely with his thumb and Wesley looks past him, as if he might see across those dark fields. "I got stuck," he says again. "It's pretty bad."

"Car?"

"Yeah." He nods, and adds, "My mom's."

"Who's your mom?"

"Koskey," he says, "Theresa. Jim and Theresa Koskey." And he shrugs the rain off his shoulders, shaking his whole body, like a dog.

"Come in," Wesley says finally, and steps back a bit so the boy can wedge himself through the door.

"Thanks. Thanks a lot. I sure do appreciate it."

The boy is panting a little, as if he had run part of the way. Wesley stares at him, trying to place him from around town, and the boy looks down, notices Wesley's bare feet, looks away, up at the coloured squares of carpet Wesley has used to insulate the entrance, at the stacks of newspaper piled neatly to the ceiling, the mousetraps baited and ready. The boy shifts his feet, wipes his nose again.

"That Theresa Venner?" Wesley asks. "Is that her?"

"Yeah," he says, running a hand across his wet chin. "That's her." The boy clears his throat.

He is scared, Wesley thinks, he is scared of me. He pulls on his wet boots while the boy stands there not looking at him, then takes a halogen flashlight off the shelf. "I got some chains," he says, and coughs. "In the barn."

And the boy, Koskey, nods without looking up. "That'd be great," he says, and stamps his muddy boots against the floor. "I surely would appreciate it," he says.

The car, one of those small foreign ones, has slid sideways down the ditch and now sits at a strange angle, the headlights pointing up into the still leafless branches of the few trees and willow scrub that line this end of the road like bones. Those lights shooting up through the trees, and Wesley thinks for a moment of that other night, when he and his father were coming back late from the lease land across the 41, slow with weariness, Wesley half-asleep against the window. Suddenly his father said, *Oh Jesus,* a whisper almost, or a choke. And Wesley sat up to see all that metal—a car maybe, was it?— bent around the front of a semi turned on its side in the ditch. *Oh, Jesus, Jesus,* and Wesley followed his father out into that impossible silence, only the sound of that one wheel spinning, *sh-sh-sh.* His father's face as he crossed the crazy bend of a headlight, that headlight across the—*Stay in the truck, Wes*— though he was in high school then, a man almost—*Stay in the truck, Wesley, for Christ's sake.*

"There she is," Koskey says now, pointing unnecessarily through the rain and the wipers.

Wesley gears down. "Should've cut the lights."

"Engine's running," Koskey says, then adds, "I got some friends with me. They should've turned the lights off. When they couldn't see me anymore. I guess they should've turned them off then. I don't know why they didn't."

Wesley backs the truck up as near as he can get to the car, grabs the chains from the box and follows the boy, sliding more than walking down the slope. When the boy opens the door and leans inside, he sees three others. A girl wearing big gold hoops in her ears hunches against a red-haired boy in the back seat. The other one, a blonde girl, sits shivering in the front, arms wrapped around her waist, long bangs looping down over her eyes. He stares a moment, wondering why she looks so strange, before he realizes that she, too, is wet. He is not stupid; he doesn't need to ask what they were doing here, out this close to the hills. But he wants to know, Why is the girl wet, did she walk, too? Did she walk part of the way and turn back?

"What's he doing here?" he hears the red-haired boy say. "Didn't you call no one?"

"He offered to pull us out." The three kids, all except the blonde one, exchange a look Wesley pretends not to notice. The girl with the earrings giggles, ducks her head so the hoops jiggle against her face.

Wesley hooks the chains to the front axle, walks back to the truck for the straw bale. Koskey follows. "I can take that for you, sir," he calls, and Wesley lets him. Pulls his jackknife out to cut the twine.

"That's a good knife," the boy says loudly, over the rain and the two engines, "that's a beauty."

Wesley snaps through the twine, folds the knife into his pants pocket, pulls away an end of the bale. "Front-wheel?" he asks.

"What?" The boy's breath puffs out in the air.

"Front-wheel drive?"

"Yeah," the boy says, "I think so. I'm pretty sure."

Wesley kneels to jam straw under the front tires, looks through the windshield, past the wipers, at the blonde girl, the suggestion of her pale face, the rain now running in a cold stream down his neck.

"Shouldn't o' spun your tires," he says to the boy. "Dug yourself deep."

The boy crams a fistful of straw under the other tire, his face down close to the mud, runs the back of his hand across his nose. He stands before answering. "Yeah," he says, "I know."

Wesley straightens, rubs straw from his wet hands.

"Your buddy willing to push?"

The boy looks doubtfully back at the car.

"Need you both."

"Yeah," he says, "he'll push."

"Somebody steering?"

The boy shrugs. "Crystal, I guess," he says. "Crystal can steer."

"Come in," Wesley says, holding the screen door. He is speaking to all of them, but it is the blonde girl he looks at, Crystal. The girl with the earrings pushes the red-haired boy in ahead of her, giggles again, but it sounds shrill and forced in the quiet house.

Wesley goes to the kitchen while they remove their shoes, fills the electric kettle with water, reaches for the jar of Nescafé. He knows they have not come in behind him; they are standing in the porch, hands jammed into the pockets of their jackets, the blonde girl farthest back.

"I guess we should call someone," Koskey says to him. "We'll need someone to come get us, I guess."

Wesley nods. "Phone's in the hall there."

The kids shift their feet and look at each other. The girl with the hoops checks her watch. "It's late," she says in a low voice to the others.

"I'm not calling Herb," the red-haired boy says. "He'll have my balls."

"You should call," the girl with the hoops says to Koskey. "It's your car."

"Herb has four-wheel," Koskey says.

"It's your car," the red-haired boy says firmly. "You were driving."

Koskey stands there a minute, deciding. He does not look at the blonde girl.

"Yeah," he says, "I guess I should call." He rubs a hand across the back of his neck and glances at Wesley. Then he goes down the hall, where they hear him pick up the phone, the slow *whirr* of the dial.

"Come in," Wesley says to the others, motioning, "sit."

The girl with the hoops perches herself on the red-haired boy's knee, hooking one arm around his neck. He shifts her on his lap, puts an arm around her waist, drops it. Wesley knows they are pretending not to look around, not to be surprised at the scrubbed counters, the neat row of canisters, the dishcloth folded lengthwise across the faucet. The new radio on top the fridge is the only thing that has changed since his mother. It is still her kitchen.

The blonde girl sits at the far end of the table, running her toe in circles around one of the silvery flecks floating in the linoleum.

"Coffee's coming," he says, placing four mugs on the table with a dish of sugar cubes and some Coffee-mate. "Here's towels. You can dry off there, in the bathroom."

The red-haired boy and the girl with the hoops both look at the blonde girl, her long hair plastered down against her jacket in peaks, as though frozen. Wesley tries not to stare at her. He keeps thinking, There is something familiar.

They can hear Koskey's voice coming low from the hallway, then the click of the receiver and he is back in the kitchen, standing in the doorway, unhappy.

"Well?" the red-haired boy asks.

"He's coming." His mouth set in a grim line. Then he adds,

half-apologetically, "He's calling Herb. For the four-wheel."

"Shit," says the red-haired boy.

They are all quiet a moment. The blonde girl looks across the table at Koskey, who stares back at her. She takes one of the towels from the table and waits.

"I know," he says finally, quietly. He looks away, rubbing his hands on his knees. The girl hesitates, then disappears down the hall.

"We sure do appreciate it," Koskey says to Wesley after she's gone.

Wesley nods. So the blonde girl is with him, then; they are a couple. He notices the girl with the earrings is wearing a dress and stockings with rhinestones on the ankle.

"Social in town tonight?" he asks.

"Yeah," Koskey says. "It was winding down."

"Right," the red-haired boy says, "winding down. You mean it was missing something." And the girl with the earrings punches him in the shoulder.

"What?" Wesley says, in spite of himself. "What was it missing?"

"Preacher's girl," the girl with the earrings says. Then adds, "Saint Crystal."

"Shut up, Janine," Koskey says.

The girl with the earrings, Janine, and the red-haired boy laugh, but they shut up. The kettle whistles and Wesley pours out water into each of the mugs. So she's a preacher's kid. Which preacher? he wonders. From town?

He stands leaning against the counter, watching them pass around the dish of sugar cubes, stir their coffees, the spoons loud against the cups. Janine takes a sip, sets her cup down. Koskey looks up at Wesley as if to say something, then back down at his cup, stirs again. Wesley thinks, There must be something I could say. But nothing comes. Only foolishness, fragments. *Rain's been a long time coming. Hill road's a real bugger in this weather. Stuck out there myself a time or two. Coffee okay? You know there was this surveyor once, Robert McCallum I think his name was, an Englishman—do you know this one?—he was a good shot and sat a horse like he was born riding one, but he wasn't used to the land here, went a little touched, some said, and took up living in a skin-tent over by Ingebrigt Lake, not much of a lake really, couple miles south of here, until one day he just disappeared, left the tent and the horse and just disappeared, nobody knows where . . .*

But he says nothing. Instead, he reaches to turn on the radio, and as he does the bathroom door opens. The blonde girl, Crystal, comes out, hair combed straight back from her face and the towel draped around her shoulders. With her face exposed like that, Wesley realizes with a twinge of surprise that he knows her, that thin, pale face, alert and birdlike, those eyes, not quite pretty. He stands with his hand on the radio dial, and in that moment he is back at the corner table of the Parrish Hotel years ago, a glass of ginger ale in its wet ring before him and all that light from a Thursday afternoon in August pouring in through the small, grimy windows. The door swings open luridly into sunlight, and a group of young people crowds in, chooses the big table next to him. Well, not that young, not too much younger than he is, probably early twenties, but not from town. He doesn't recognize them. One of the girls elbows her friend, lifts her chin in his direction, and they both laugh. It's nothing, really, just kids being silly. But he pulls out his wallet anyway, counts the change for his pop, carefully, until he feels someone standing at his elbow. It is the girl from the next table, grinning, her hair frizzed out, her teeth pointy, like a cat's. She looks back once over her shoulder, giggles, and says, "So sorry to bother you, but someone over there thinks you're really cute. Her, right there in the yellow blouse." She points back to a blonde girl he does not recognize, sitting shrunk in her chair, miserable. He meets the girl's eyes for just a second, sees she is humiliated, sorry for them both. Even from where he sits, he can see a small round scar on her chin—it is nothing, but he feels at that moment as if it is the saddest thing he's ever seen. The girl looks down, letting her blonde hair swing over her eyes. He knows he should feel humiliated, too; the joke is on him, after all. But he wishes she would look up, wishes he could catch her eye again, let her know somehow this kind of thing doesn't matter. He would smile and nod, hoping she knew that he realized it was a joke, knowing somehow she would understand. "She says she'd like to be your girlfriend," says the girl with the pointy teeth. "Wouldn't you, Clare?"

Clare. Of course. He'd forgotten all about her. Clare. He steals a glance at the blonde girl hunched over his table. How odd, he thinks, how odd to think that I knew her, as if time had collapsed for that second. This girl is maybe fifteen, sixteen. Clare would be, what? Forty now? Older?

He feels ashamed, then, as if he has spoken his error aloud, as if they all know. But they just sit at the table, sipping their coffee, waiting for their parents to collect them, parents he probably knew at school, though they would have been younger, maybe, parents he still sees sometimes on his infrequent visits to town, where they greet him in the feed store, slap him on the shoulder and bark, "Hey there, Wes, you still living the bachelor's life out there? That's the way, boy, that's the way. You ain't missing a thing, buddy. You got it all figured out, but what I want to know is why the hell didn't you tell the rest of us sorry sonsabitches before it was too late?" And they all guffaw and he ducks his head good-naturedly and says, "Yeah, that's for sure, eh? That's right."

"They're here," Koskey says now, and Wesley turns to see truck lights pull into the yard. None of the kids move. They sit there at his table, not looking at each other, not looking at him—except for the blonde girl who, for the first time, stares straight at him, her face blank with fear, and he remembers: preacher's kid. She's probably not supposed to be here at all. She stares at him, as if he could do something to fix things, as if willing an assurance from him, sits there small and shivering again under the damp towel. He sees she is even smaller than he thought. Here, in the light of the kitchen, with her hair combed back, she is a child. And he thinks, There is very little resemblance really.

Outside, the horn blows once, long and hard.

"Well," Koskey says, rising first, "I guess this is it."

Wesley watches them file out to the porch and pull on their shoes slowly. He wonders whether he should walk them out to the truck, but it is raining still. And he realizes then that he is wearing his wet shirt, realizes he is freezing. He shouldn't go out again. It wouldn't be smart, getting a chill. He is not as young as he used to be.

"Thanks again," Koskey yells, as they run out the door into the rain. The blonde girl is the last to go. In the dimness of the porch, she is not Crystal, but Clare again. He almost asks, "Who's your mother?" Almost. And then he thinks, What does it matter? Even if it was so, what would I say to her? "I knew your mother once, just for a second. I knew her." No, he would only frighten the girl. But she turns to him then, hands him the towel from around her neck. "It's not what you think," she says. "Nothing happened." As if it mattered, what he thought. Her face is wet, maybe from the rain. And then she is outside, walking straight into the headlights, the rain bouncing from the shoulders of her jacket.

He thinks he should follow her. Go out and say hello at least to the parents. But he doesn't. He closes the door and steps back into the kitchen, lifts his coffee to his lips and gulps hugely, letting the hot liquid warm his throat, his chest. He wraps his hands around the cup the way his mother used to in the evenings at the kitchen table with his father, and for years after his father was gone, just the two of them, remembering him, until at last she was too old to remember. And then she was gone, too.

And he thinks, No, this is not right. I should go out there, step through those headlights and the rain. I should say hello at least. I could do that much. Though he really means, *I could do that much for her, for the girl. I could say something. It's not what you think, boys. Nothing happened.* So he sets down his cup and pulls his boots on over his bare feet, ducks out onto the porch steps. But they have gone, the red brake lights blinking once and then turning out past the caraganas, the back end of the truck fish-tailing in the mud. He stands there with the rain piercing his bones, listening to the sound of the engine recede into the night, thinking he is not as young as he used to be. Thinking it wouldn't have mattered anyway. And he thinks, There is this girl, Crystal, and there was another girl once, Clare. That is all. Clare. With blonde hair and a scar on her chin. There was that, at least. He could remember that kind of thing; he could remember that still.

Small Comfort

The summer Cora Mae Clark and her brother Boyd turned up, I'd only just kicked my habit of sleeping with a night light—a painful adjustment, learning to fall asleep with all that darkness edging up against me. But I would never have admitted that to Cora Mae, not with her tight smile, the fearless blonde arch of her eyebrows. She wasn't the sort of girl you confided in. Not about something like a night light anyway. And Boyd . . . well, Boyd was something else entirely.

He was three years older than I was and almost two years older than Cora Mae, though you never would have guessed it to look at them. Despite his advantage of height, a certain looseness about his limbs made him seem younger, as if he had not yet gained control of his muscles, as if he could shoot off in any direction without warning at any time. Not just adolescent gawkiness; he lived in perpetual erratic motion. Next to the neat, precise, oddly adult movements of Cora Mae's compact body, Boyd was like some clumsy marionette, capable of sudden bursts of absurd energy.

"That's just Boyd," Cora Mae sighed that first day, "trying to get attention. Ignore him."

I watched him from the concrete steps outside the Lucky Dollar grocery store where I waited for my mother. It seemed to me that getting attention hardly interested Boyd. He sat hunched over something halfway down the block, at the mouth of one of those weedy little alleys that ran between the few buildings on Main Street, rocking back and forth on his heels, fluttering his hands in quick, nervous movements. There was a certain fragility in the way all his parts seemed to work, or not to work, in unison, as if a puff of wind could easily collapse him. As I watched, he stood up, crouched down, stood up again, his feet tapping, his whole body quivering.

"Cora Mae," he called back over his shoulder, waving a white hand, "c'mere."

Cora Mae bent to rub a smudge of dust off the top of her sandal. Then she straightened with decisive grace and looked down at me, wrinkling her sunburned nose. "I used to have a barrette like that."

The plastic butterfly I'd used to jam my overgrown bangs from my face was an old yellow one, part of a set I'd received several Christmases ago when my mother began selling Avon. I raised my fingers, flushing with embarrassment as I touched the rough corner where I'd chewed most of one wing away.

"We're staying with my Uncle Alec," Cora Mae said gaily. "For a week. Our parents are in Florida. They're always some-where." Then, unnecessarily, "We don't live here, of course," looking up and down the wide, bald expanse of Main Street—empty, except for us—with an expression of semi-amused won-der that anyone could. I hoped Barney Burkenchuk would not that moment drive his tractor down Main Street, as he some-times did.

"You want some gum?" she asked, thrusting a pack under my nose.

I did but said no anyway, staring at my thongs, worn to a thin edge at the heel, and at the jagged curves of my toenails. "You could gut a fish with those," my mother had quipped the night before. Ever since she'd started selling Avon, she'd thought of me as a kind of walking advertisement for what she called the junior miss products: creme rinse and talcum powder and those little plastic brooches with scented pomade inside, the ones shaped like animals. I eyed Cora Mae's white sandals. They had a bit of a heel. Hardly any girls in town wore white sandals. None wore heels. "They're just not practical, Audrey," my mother would say, sniffing. "Grooming, now that's what tells. It wouldn't kill you to wear a little lip gloss." Cora Mae's toes poked from the tips of her sandals, nails trimmed into neat pink squares. I slid my feet under me on the step and turned partially away, pretending to peer off at something interesting in the distance. I thought Cora Mae might take the hint and leave, but instead she flashed her hand in front of my face.

"Ever seen a mood ring?" she asked. "They're the latest. It changes colour depending on your mood. See? Light green. That means I'm calm." She turned her hand so the sun caught the silver setting. "My boyfriend gave it to me," she said, and sighed. "*Ex*-boyfriend." She twisted the ring off and handed it to me. "Here, you try."

I hesitated. I could tell it would be too small. "You have your father's hands," my mother was fond of saying, "literally."

"It's okay," Cora Mae said, misreading my hesitation. "We broke up." She looked critically at my hands and added, "Try it on the pinky. It doesn't matter—your mood's the same in every finger."

She squished the ring onto my pinky, and we sat staring at

my hand propped awkwardly against my knee. I wondered if Cora Mae noticed how the skin dried in white cracks across my kneecaps. "Moisturize," my mother would say, "moisturize."

"You have to wait a while," Cora Mae said, and tapped her sandal against the concrete.

"Cora Mae," Boyd called again, "hey." This time, neither of us looked.

"There. See?" she said. "It's changing." It was. Darkening against my hand like a beetle. "Purple!" she cried. "For passion."

I tried to slide the ring off my finger. "Purple," Cora Mae repeated in a breathy voice as I bent my head, trying to hide the fact that I was twisting the ring mercilessly. "That's rare. It hardly ever turns purple. You must be in love. Are you in love?"

I briefly considered the boys from town.

Cora Mae tapped my hand. "Don't worry about that. You can get it off with baby oil."

"Oh." I didn't know what else to say. "Okay." I kept twisting anyway, but discreetly, hoping she wouldn't notice. I had begun to sweat and thought, optimistically, it might help.

"You shouldn't do that," Cora Mae said. "It looks like your finger's swelling a bit."

It was a relief when Boyd's pale, tense face appeared over his sister's shoulder. "Hey, Cora Mae," he said, "look what I got." He offered his cupped palms.

"So," said Cora Mae, picking a piece of lint from her skirt. "A dead bird."

"It's not dead," Boyd said, "just hurt."

I stood up to look closer. "It's a meadowlark," I said.

"Yeah." Boyd stroked the bird gently with his thumb. "I know. Young. A female. You can tell by the colourings. There's not much yellow. See?" I had not known there was any difference. The bird looked like any old meadowlark to me, but I leaned in closer, pretending to examine it. Boyd shifted his feet, as if anxious to go somewhere. "You think they'd give me a box?" he asked, looking up at the store.

"You can't take a bird in there," Cora Mae said. "It's probably got lice or something."

I had to agree. My mother alone would have at least one fit at the sight of it. "I could go see," I offered.

Boyd hesitated, bouncing a little on the balls of his feet. "Okay, sure," he said finally, "but not too big. About the size of a shoebox maybe. With a lid."

"Do you always have to make a *scene*?" I heard Cora Mae say as I swung through the door, thongs slapping.

My mother stood at the counter talking to Elise Halson, who worked the cash. I didn't know her well—she'd graduated the year before and then gone away to beauty college in Medicine Hat—but I still admired her with that mixture of fear and awe reserved for all the high school girls. She was leaning with one hand on the cash register, the other hooked in the back pocket of her jeans.

"All I'm saying," my mother was whispering, "is it's time he grew up. She's already got three kids—she doesn't need a fourth." As soon as she noticed me, she hooked my arm and pulled me over.

"Here," she said to Elise, "you see?" I winced as she snapped the barrette from my hair and scooted my bangs over my face. "You see? If you could just give her something shorter, something . . . perky. For the summer."

"Sure thing," Elise said, flicking judiciously at my bangs. "That's a cinch."

I brushed the hair out of my eyes and noticed Elise was looking past me.

"Can I help you?" she asked.

Cora Mae, standing just inside the door, looked at me, then

back at Elise. "I wanted to see about the box for my brother," she said politely. "Please."

"You need a box," my mother said, "for your brother?"

"For his bird," I said, sticking my barrette in my pocket.

"He's not bringing it in here, I hope." My mother craned her neck toward the door. Boyd pressed his face to the glass. She frowned. "Is that him?"

"A small one," I said to Elise, "but with a lid."

"Sure thing," she said, unhooking her hand from her jeans pocket and rummaging under the counter. Her T-shirt had a big pink heart with *Foxy Lady* written across the centre in silver glitter that had flecked off in places.

The three of us stood waiting.

"So, Audrey," my mother said finally, beaming at Cora Mae, "who's your friend?"

"It's nice to see you *socialize* more," my mother called through the open kitchen window. "I can't stand your lurking around the house all summer. It gives me the creeps. I hope you changed your shirt."

I was slumped against the front steps waiting for Cora Mae. My mother had invited her. I was hoping Boyd would come, too, though the invitation had not included him. "*She* gives me the creeps," I said, meaning Cora Mae.

"Don't be silly," my mother said, and closed the window.

I spotted them as soon as they turned the corner, Cora Mae several brisk steps ahead, yellow skirt swishing, Boyd trailing behind, balancing as carefully as a fishbowl the mandarin orange crate Elise had given him. I straightened, rubbed dirt from my hands where I'd been idly digging, with a degree of undisguised resentment, in one of my mother's flowerpots.

"I told him not to bring the bird," Cora Mae grumbled as she came up our sidewalk.

"That's okay."

Boyd minced his way across the lawn delicately, as if walking on tiptoe. It looked funny, but I didn't laugh. I walked down the steps and sat on the grass. Cora Mae joined me, but Boyd stayed by the cotoneaster hedges, tucking his box gently in the shade. He had on the same pair of brown corduroy pants and light blue T-shirt he'd been wearing the day before, and for some reason this made me like him immensely. He opened the lid and bent over the box, speaking earnestly.

"He thinks he can teach that bird to talk," Cora Mae snorted. "That's pretty stupid. Don't you think?"

I knew you couldn't teach a meadowlark to talk. At least, I didn't think it was likely.

"I guess."

"Trust me," she said. "It's stupid." She leaned back, propping herself on her elbows. "He's in for a surprise next year, though. They don't let a person get away with that kind of thing in high school."

"High school?"

"Yeah," she said, plucking at the bands of her white knee socks. "They skipped him ahead. He should only be in eighth."

High school. I could hardly imagine it, could hardly imagine Boyd with his skinny arms and quick, nervous gestures circulating in that realm populated by Elise Halsons in *Foxy Lady* T-shirts. I couldn't picture him there any more than I could picture myself. I looked again where he crouched by the orange crate, collecting cotoneaster leaves in fat bunches. And then I thought, Why not a meadowlark? If some birds can talk, why not others? Why not a meadowlark?

"You have dirt on your knees," Cora Mae said.

I licked my fingers and rubbed. Then we both sat silent, watching Boyd, listening to the faint buzz of a lawn mower down the street.

My mother tapped on the glass of the kitchen window and waved cheerily, then glanced suspiciously toward Boyd before disappearing.

"She seems nice," Cora Mae said.

"Mmm-hmm."

I slipped my thongs off, noticed the rim of dirt around my soles, slipped them back on again.

"Anyway," Cora Mae said, nodding toward Boyd, "he just does it to get attention. He's not half as sick as they say he is."

"He's sick?" I said. I looked at him. He didn't look sick. "What's the matter with him?"

"Nothing," Cora Mae snapped. "It's all up here." She tapped a finger to the side of her head. "If you know what I mean."

I didn't, but did not say so. I felt uneasy with the subject, with the way Cora Mae talked as if we were old friends. She reminded me, in some weird way, of my mother, of the way she and her friends exchanged confidences over coffee, making thinly veiled allusions to matters of an intimate nature.

"Anyway," Cora Mae said again, after a while, "I could care less. I'm changing schools this year. That's exciting, don't you think?"

"What are you changing schools for?"

She shrugged. "Just for a change," she said.

She scowled and stretched her legs in the grass. I noticed with a touch of alarm that they were covered in a soft blonde fuzz, like the skin of a peach.

"I have to go," I said abruptly. "I have an appointment." It wasn't a lie, not really. I was supposed to be at Elise's for a haircut by three-thirty. It couldn't have been much past one. "Here's your ring," I said, digging in my pocket.

Cora Mae looked genuinely disappointed. "What kind of appointment?"

I held out the ring but kept it low, away from her face; it still had a fatty smell from the lard I'd used to squeeze it off my finger. Some had seeped into the setting, though I'd tried to dig most of it out with a toothpick.

"It's way on the other side of town."

"Oh," Cora Mae said, standing up. "We can walk you."

I got up reluctantly, brushed grass from the back of my shorts. "Here," I said, pushing the ring at her.

"You keep it," she said. "I'm kind of sick of it anyway."

I both did and did not want it, but she'd already turned away, so I stuck it back in my pocket, thinking she'd probably ask for it later. Maybe by then the lard smell would have worn off.

"Come on, Boyd," Cora Mae said. Without asking where we were going, he carefully packed up the crate and followed. Cora Mae walked quickly, purposefully, as if she was the one with the appointment, and Boyd trailed behind, weaving from the sidewalk to the pavement and back again. I dragged my heels, too, partly because it was only a fifteen-minute walk at most, even though Elise did live on the other side of town, partly because I was hoping Boyd would catch up.

"How's the bird?" I asked him.

His face looked grim. "I don't know. She doesn't seem much better. I thought it was her wing, but it seems worse than that."

"Like what?" I asked.

"So what's there to do around here anyway?" Cora Mae interrupted.

I considered. There was the five-pin bowling alley, Dan's Café, the swimming pool, though that hadn't yet opened for the summer. There was the river, though I was certain Cora Mae wouldn't set foot in that brown, swirling water. Besides, there was always the risk it might get back to my mother, who had forbidden me even to approach its muddy banks. That left the Sand Hills, the only other place visitors to town ever seemed to want to go. "If you haven't seen the Sand Hills," my mother would tell them, "you haven't seen Saskatchewan." And she would happily drive them out, bumping the car along the narrow prairie trail, then stop and point from the window, tapping a long fingernail against the glass. "There," she'd say, "isn't that something, now." And the visitors would ask if they could get out, walk around a bit, take a closer look. "Oh," she'd say, "you *could*," and then wrinkle her nose to imply that it was best just to admire from the car.

"There's the Sand Hills," I said. "My mom might drive us."

"Oh," Cora Mae said drily, "we've seen those."

"Uncle Alec and Aunt Marion took us," Boyd piped up behind. "It was amazing. Just like a desert, all those ripples in the sand. It must go for miles."

"Is that your school?" Cora Mae said, pointing ahead.

I nodded, embarrassed by the bland flat-roofed building, the weeds in the dusty playground. I hadn't been there since classes let out, and it looked much smaller than I remembered.

"Uncle Alec said all the kids in town go there, from grade one right to twelve."

Actually, kindergarten to twelve, but I didn't tell Cora Mae that. I kicked at a stone in the road and it pinged against a metal fence post.

"Everybody?" Boyd asked. I was walking so slowly he couldn't help but catch up. Even when he was poking along like that, there was still something erratic about his movements, a potential for disaster. He reminded me of that party game my parents sometimes played when, well into the first bottle of rye, they'd fill a cookie sheet with water and take turns with their friends racing haphazardly across the living room, shrieking with laughter. I always thought there had to be more to that game than I was seeing. Boyd reminded me of that. Intensity and lack of control and some other element I couldn't quite put my finger on. I kept watching him, thinking, He's going to drop that box any minute.

"Everybody?" he asked again.

"Everybody what?"

"Goes to the same school?"

"We're not all in the same room or anything," I said. "The high school is down at one end and the little kids at the other. *Way* at the other."

"And you're in the middle," Boyd said.

Actually, the grade five classroom was pretty much at the little kids' end, so I didn't say anything. It wasn't exactly a question anyway.

"That must be terrible," Cora Mae sympathized.

I hadn't really thought about it. It wasn't terrible. It just was.

But before I could answer, Boyd said, apparently without animosity, "Cora Mae doesn't understand the meaning of terrible."

Her face stiffened. "What do you know?" she said, voice low.

"I'm just saying there's nothing terrible about that. I think it's pretty amazing. Just think."

"Just think of what?" I asked. Cora Mae was walking a few steps ahead of us, shoulders braced. She did not turn around.

Boyd stopped in the road and stared at me. "Why, the potential for"—he lifted the box slightly—"for all kinds of things."

The Halsons lived at the new end of town, on the last street before Old Man Cassel's summerfallow field. My mother always said you couldn't pay her to live over there, not even for one of those "new" (she always used her fingers here to make quotation marks in the air) houses. "Too much wind," she said. "And you get all the dust. Who needs it?"

The Halsons had the very last lot on the block, which meant they were bordered on one side by Cassel's summerfallow and on the other by what I called the pond: really just a deep slough frequented by ducks, frogs and salamanders and covered with a spongy layer of lime-coloured algae that smelled in summer. There were rumours of rattlers, but I'd never seen one. I'd always been envious of Elise's proximity to the pond. It seemed a kind of status symbol, like having a swimming pool in your backyard. I doubted that she appreciated it, doubted whether she valued, as I would have, the slow croaking of frogs through her bedroom window on summer nights. She didn't seem the type.

"I thought you were getting a haircut," Cora Mae said sulkily. She had not spoken since the schoolyard.

"I am."

"At someone's *house*?"

"She has a diploma," I said, just in case Cora Mae imagined some grandma hacking at my hair around the edge of a soup bowl. "From Medicine Hat."

"Why doesn't she have a salon, then?"

I shrugged. Cora Mae looked skeptical as the three of us filed into the backyard, where we found Elise reclined in a lawn chair, flipping the pages of a haircutting magazine. She wore a tight yellow tank top with spaghetti straps and cut-off shorts rolled as high as they would go. Cora Mae brightened at the sight of her.

"Wow," Elise said, "you're early. Your mom said three-thirty, right?"

I nodded, aware that Cora Mae had come up beside me and

was beaming at Elise. Much to my surprise, she took my hand. I couldn't see Boyd, but I sensed his movements somewhere behind us.

"I guess that's okay," Elise said, closing her magazine. She squinted at us. "Are your friends staying?"

Cora Mae piped up, "I'm going to take hairdressing when I graduate. It's the neatest."

"Well," Elise said modestly, "I'm still pretty new at it." She looked at Boyd, who was pacing up and down the sidewalk.

"That's just Boyd," Cora Mae said. "He'll wait outside."

"Okay." Elise said. "Whatever." She led us to the back door. Cora Mae had dropped my hand and was at Elise's heels in a flash. I hesitated, looking back at Boyd. "If you leave the bird out here," I said, "you can probably come in, too."

Boyd glanced at me briefly. "What for?"

I couldn't really say, so I left him under Mrs. Halson's gooseberry bushes and followed Elise and Cora Mae inside.

"Down here," Elise called as I closed the door behind me. The house had a faint sweet odour, like overripe fruit, and all the blinds were drawn against the afternoon sun. I slipped off my thongs, imagining it was expected, and went downstairs.

Though the basement had no windows to speak of, it was brighter, lit by two bare overhead bulbs. Cora Mae was already posed primly on an old vinyl chesterfield next to a sink and an odd contraption on cinder blocks that looked as if it might once have been a tractor seat. The rest of the basement consisted of a concrete floor and fibreglass insulation running up the unfinished walls. Behind the chesterfield and the sink, Elise had hung old blankets and sheets and had rolled out a section of purple shag carpet across the floor. "For ambience," she said. A battered dresser with jars, combs, scissors and sprays, two large hand-held mirrors and a vase of silk flowers stood in front of the chair. In one corner was a stereo, where

Elise stood flipping through albums. Above it hung a poster of horses running across a misty field.

"I like to play a little music when I work," she explained. "It relaxes the customers."

I sat on the chesterfield next to Cora Mae.

Elise slipped a record from its sheath. "Have you heard this one?" She dropped the needle and swayed her hips with the opening notes. "It's Barbra Streisand."

"Oh," Cora Mae said, "I love this one."

"Yeah," Elise said. "Me, too. I love it."

"Don't you just love it?" Cora Mae said to me.

"Did you see the movie?" Elise asked. "I loved it."

I shifted away from a spring that was digging into the back of my leg and watched with unease as Elise sang, "*Ev-er-greeeen.*"

"This is the song I'll have played at my wedding," she said. "Here, listen to this." And she turned the volume up. "This is the best part."

I felt hot and embarrassed, unable to look at Elise sliding her feet across the purple carpet. Instead, I stared at the poster of the horses. It read in elaborate script across the bottom: *If you love something, set it free. If it comes back, it's yours. If it doesn't, it never was meant to be.* The backs of my thighs stuck wetly to the vinyl chesterfield, and my skin pinched each time I shifted. I was beginning to feel as if something would be required of me.

"Can I use your bathroom?" I blurted.

Elise stopped swaying and opened her eyes. She turned the volume down a little. "What?"

"Can I use your bathroom?" I repeated. This time I was careful to suppress the panic in my voice.

"Yeah," Elise said, motioning vaguely. "Upstairs, through the kitchen." She took the record off and slid a new one on the turntable. "How about this?"

"Ooh," Cora Mae said. "I love this one."

"Me, too," I heard Elise say as I headed up the stairs. "I really love it."

Boyd had gone down to the pond. I could just make out his blue T-shirt among the cattail reeds. I stepped into my thongs and slipped out the door.

"What are you looking at?" I asked, my feet sinking in the wet bank.

"Tadpoles," he said, without turning around. "There's a lot of them." The orange crate sat open at his feet and I peered inside.

"Hey," I said, alarmed. "The bird's gone."

Boyd picked up a stick and poked it into the water, swishing it back and forth.

"Boyd," I said, lifting the crate and looking quickly around, "your bird's gone."

"I know." He stood up and walked farther down the bank toward a cluster of ducks.

I followed, feet squelching, the cardboard orange crate bumping against my legs, and stopped next to where he stood watching the ducks bob their slick heads and resurface, bodies quivering.

"Those ones over there"—Boyd pointed—"those are mallards. That's a drake. See the green?"

"What about the purple ones?" I asked, though I didn't really care. I wanted to know what had happened to the meadowlark.

"Those are drakes, too," he said. "Teals, I think. Females don't have those colours. They're the brown ones. It's like that with most bird species."

"Why?" I asked.

"Mating mostly," he said. "The males use their colour to attract a mate. And the females are brownish so they blend in with the ground and the grass and stuff. For nesting."

I sat on a rock and settled the orange crate at my feet. Boyd paced the bank of the pond, pointing at various things with his stick. After a while he stopped talking and stood quietly again, just staring over the water. I'd never seen him still before. But I didn't get a sense of peace from his stillness. It made me uneasy.

"I didn't get a haircut," I ventured. "I guess my mom'll be pretty mad."

"You were supposed to get a haircut?"

"Yeah." I shrugged. "It was my mom's idea. She'll be pretty mad, I guess."

He turned around and squinted at me. "I can cut it for you."

I was doubtful. "You can?"

"Sure," he said, pulling a folding knife from his pants pocket. "I cut my own all the time. It's easy."

I squirmed a little at the sight of the fine blade glinting in the sun. "Does that work?"

"I just said so, didn't I?" He pointed the blade at me. "Here. Feel how sharp it is."

When I didn't move, he poked it closer. I touched a finger against the edge of the blade, just barely. It was sharp, all right.

"See?" he said, twisting a chunk of his hair. "You just take it like this and saw at it like so." He made a sawing motion in the air. "Easy."

I looked at the knife again, then at Boyd's hair. It didn't look any different from any other boy's. "Well . . ." I hesitated.

"We can start at the back, where it's longest," he said sensibly. "That way, if anything goes wrong, the rest of your hair will hide it."

I looked over my shoulder toward the house, wondered if Elise and Cora Mae had even noticed I'd gone. "Okay," I said, taking a big breath and dipping my head as though going underwater.

He started, as he'd said, at the back. I'd expected it to hurt a little, but the sensation was more like a persistent tugging at my scalp. I thought uneasily of that blade so close to my body. After all, I hardly knew this boy. Didn't know him at all. But Boyd worked silently, efficiently, directing me with single-word commands, *tilt, lift,* and I soon relaxed into the pleasurable feel of his hands in my hair, as if I were being stroked peacefully into sleep.

He finished in no time. I ran my hands across my head, felt a strange sort of dizzy elatedness.

"There," Boyd said, stepping back to admire his work. "I cut it really short. That way you don't have to do it again for a while."

I kept running my hands over my head, loving the feel of it. Like the fur of some small animal.

"Does it look like yours?" I asked.

He cocked his head to one side. "Yeah," he said, flipping the blade shut, "pretty much."

I was pleased. Boyd bent to gather the long hanks of hair in the mud around the rock. "Want this?" he asked.

"What for?"

"I don't know," he said. "To make things. Hair's good for nests, especially. Or whatever. It's not just dead cells. Not really."

"What is it?"

He spoke slowly, thinking. "It's . . . I don't know. But there's something in it. Something like your soul. That's why there's so many myths about it. Samson. Rapunzel. Medusa, even."

Rapunzel, at least, I knew. He handed me the hair he'd collected, but I shook my head. "You can have it," I offered, "if you want." I didn't believe that stuff about soul.

"Really?" he said. "I never get this much of my own." He picked up the orange crate and stuffed my hair inside. It was strange to know he would take it with him somewhere.

"Boyd," I said quietly, "what happened to the bird?"

He kept his head bent, as if he hadn't heard me, and fiddled with the lid of the box. Out on the pond there was a quick flapping and splashing of wings, and I imagined, without looking, a duck landing.

"Did you let her go?" I asked. "Was she better?"

I didn't meet either Boyd or Cora Mae the rest of that week, half to my disappointment and half not. It was Boyd I wanted to see, of course, but Cora Mae filled me with near dread. I spent my afternoons concocting impossible plans for getting to Boyd without Cora Mae. I kept thinking I'd run into him somewhere around town, but I never did. In fact, I saw him only once, from a distance, as my mother and I were driving out of town. He was down by the pond behind the Halsons', pacing the bank in quick steps, arms raised, swinging a stick across the water in broad strokes, like a wizard. "That boy is so strange," my mother said, though I hadn't even told her about the haircut, had taken the blame entirely upon myself for that. "I don't want you playing with him."

I made a point of walking by the pond several times that week, but either Boyd had not come back or my timing was off, for I did not see him again. I thought I'd seen the last of Cora Mae, too, but on the Sunday they were supposed to leave, she stopped by my house. Her blonde hair was twisted back in two French braids that made her look old—not older, just old. I came out on the steps to greet her.

"Hi," she said, beaming as though we'd seen each other every day that week, "I came to say *au revoir*." I half expected some comment on my haircut or my disappearance that day at the Halsons', but she said nothing.

"You probably want this back," I said, holding out her mood ring. It no longer smelled like lard, not as much anyway.

She looked surprised. "No," she said, shaking her braids, "I gave it to you. So you have something to remember me by."

"Oh," I said, wondering if that meant I was supposed to give her something in return. All I could think of was the butterfly barrette in my pocket.

Cora Mae shifted her feet on the steps, and we both stood there uncomfortably. I looked across the yard to the two younger neighbour girls running through the sprinkler.

"Kids." Cora Mae shook her head again.

"Yeah."

"Well," she said, "I guess I should go. Why don't you give me your address? We can be pen pals or something."

"Okay." I went inside to get a pen and paper.

When I returned, Cora Mae was seated on the bottom step, knees together, staring at the neighbour kids with something that looked almost like wonder—almost, but not quite. And I felt sorry, then, in the safety of her leaving, that I had not made more of an effort to befriend her.

"Here." I handed her the paper. And then, casually, "Where's Boyd?"

For a moment, she looked hurt, just as she had that day by the schoolyard. But then she shrugged and said, too gaily, "You know Boyd!" I stood there, scratching stupidly at a mosquito bite that had scabbed over on my elbow, wondering why he had not come to say goodbye, but knowing the answer: *What for?*

"Well," Cora Mae said, rising with that unmistakable poise, "I guess I'll be going. I'll write. But you have to write back." I nodded as she swished off down the street, her sandals clicking against the hot concrete. At the corner, she turned briefly and waved. *"Au revoir!"* she shouted. And then she was gone.

It wasn't until my senior year of high school that I really thought of Cora Mae and Boyd again. Cora Mae had written twice after she'd left town that summer, but I felt I couldn't live up to the stylish, looping writing, the purple ink, the *i*'s dotted with circles instead of points. I never wrote back. I didn't really have anything to say anyway. And Boyd, well, I thought of him, of course. Quite a bit the first few months after they left. I couldn't shake the feel of his hands, so detached and efficient, moving through my hair. Once, I caught myself writing his name in the back of my math scribbler. I got a strange kind of comfort knowing he was somewhere in the world. I was curious about what he had done with my hair, if he still had it. But as the months passed, I thought of him less and wondered just briefly the following summer whether they would return. They didn't, and I soon forgot them almost entirely. By then, I'd found other friends, other interests. I say almost entirely because I could not forget that glimpse of Boyd down by the pond, his thin, nervous arms stretched wide across the water.

So when my mother returned from the coffee shop one afternoon just before graduation to tell me Cora Mae was in town, it was Boyd I thought of first.

"Oh, Audrey," my mother said in that dramatic way she had, "you should see her. To think she could let herself go like that. All that makeup, and her skin such a mess. She bleaches her hair now. It looks terrible, of course. And I always thought so highly of her. I told Alec and Marion so. I was sorry she never came back to stay with them. I always thought she would

have made a good companion for you. But to look at her now
. . ." She shook her head.

I was stretched out on my bed, doodling in my biology textbook. "Who?" I asked.

"Why, Cora Mae. That's what I've been saying. You
remember Cora Mae."

For a few seconds, I didn't, but then the name clicked.
"What about her?" I asked.

"Exactly what I've been telling you," my mother said,
plumping my pillows. "She's come to stay with Alec and
Marion. Problems at home, I think. And to look at her, I can
believe it. But they've had a hard time, that family. Alcohol
and drugs and God knows what all. It's no wonder." She
sighed. "Such a shame. She was a delightful little girl. You
should just see her now."

Try as I might, I could not imagine Cora Mae looking any
different from what I remembered, could not picture her as an
adult. To me, she'd seemed an adult back then.

"What about her brother?" I finally asked. "Boyd."

My mother stared at me blankly, as if she'd never heard of
him. "Boyd?"

"Yes," I said, annoyed, "the one with the bird. Skinny kid,
always moving."

"Yes," she said, "I know who you *mean*." She began shifting
perfume bottles into alignment on my dresser.

"Well," I said, flipping my textbook shut, "is he here, too?"

"Audrey," she said, as if I'd suddenly gone stupid, "he died.
That was ages ago."

Her words did not immediately register. I stared at her.

"Lord," she said, brushing dust from the dresser with the
palm of her hand, "that was years ago. I'm sure I told you."

I looked down at the cover of the book before me, tried to
make sense of the words, but they seemed foreign and obscure.

An unexpected stillness seemed to descend over the room, my own body.

"Audrey," my mother was saying, "I'm sure I told you. There was all that hush-hush about it, of course. An accident, they said, but I told you long ago that boy was strange. He always was. I could have told you back then he'd come to no good. Cora Mae, now, that's a real how-do-you-do. But I always say, it comes down to the parents." And she shook her head. "I *know* I told you," she said again, moving toward the door. "Anyway," I heard her call from the hallway, "I need you to run downtown. I forgot milk."

Bloodwood

At age seventy-one, Perpetua Resch could honestly say she had loved only four people: her mother, her father, her brother Martin and her sister Magda. At one time she had hoped to include Joe, but she had long since recognized this idea as the romantic illusion of a teenaged bride and the expectation attached to a young and promising marriage. This was not to say she felt no affection for her husband. On the contrary, she was very fond of him. Over the years, there had been almost nothing to complain of about Joe. The worst she could think to say was that he tended toward complacency. But even this characteristic was a minor flaw given his easy nature, his generosity and, of course, his patient and seemingly unwavering capacity for love. But to speak in terms of loving him in return . . . no, she had none of that fierce blood-rush of feeling that could thrum music from the rib cage and swell one's throat to bursting, as though it contained some beautiful, terrible balloon. Though she knew she would rather not do without Joe, she suspected that she could certainly make the adjustment with little emotional strain. Once, long ago, in a tender moment (there was a moon, she remembers), Joe had said to her, "Don't you ever die on me first. I don't know what I'd do without you." And she'd looked into his shining eyes, so pleasantly dark, and thought, *Well, all right,* even though she knew her heart should have wrenched at the thought of living without him. Oddly, she had not felt dismayed to discover, early on in marriage, the truth about her feelings for Joe. After all, it was not particularly rare in those days to be married to someone you did not love. Not unusual at all. So she had waited, instead, for the arrival of children to kindle the sort of love she knew she could expect with some degree of certainty from motherhood. When it became clear that the long-awaited arrival was not to come, Perpetua suspected that the number of those she could say she had truly loved would remain limited to four. And she briefly grieved.

Perpetua's inability to love Joe (or anyone else she had met—there had certainly been opportunities) was the result of a too-happy childhood; this she knew. Looking back, she recalled none of the petty tensions and jealousies, none of the potentially grave, deep-rooted resentments that she knew sprouted in other families. There had been quarrels and sometimes tears, even the occasional fit of temper (Martin, once, after an argument with their father—Perpetua could not now remember over what—had broken his knuckle taking a swing at the barn wall), but these had been rare and short-lived and, once past, entirely forgotten. What made possible these easy family relations, she could not suppose. But the lack of conflict and strife neither amazed nor puzzled her—after all, her own marriage had rolled along easily for fifty-five years. Rather, it was the absolute, unshakeably deep love that Magda and Martin and Perpetua and their mother and father had all seemed to feel for one another, and only for one another. Even now, when she conjured up an image of Martin, sickly always, with his too-skinny legs, walking to school through ditches bloated yellow with buffalo beans, or the unbeautiful Magda coaxing a kitten to take milk from a saucer in the little sunless back porch, she felt that huge swelling of her heart, at once so agonizing and so tender. And she was keenly aware, yet again, that she had never once had this feeling for Joe.

She liked to believe Joe had never known. She had certainly always done her best to conceal it from him. She had cooked his meals and washed his clothes and once, before they were married, when all things still seemed possible, she had danced with him under the stars on a summer night choked with the scent of hot sand and wolf willow and sage. She had held his hand and changed his sour sheets when he lay delirious with rheumatic fever, she had worked beside him in the field and in the corrals, and they had prayed every Sunday shoulder to shoulder in the little church at Johnsborough. She had lain next to him each night, peaceful or tired, sometimes angry. She had stayed, after all. And been happy, more or less. Back then, she had still had Magda and Martin and, for a few years after her mother's death, her father. And that had been enough.

Perpetua supposed her parents were to blame. Somehow, they had produced a tight iron band of love that could not be expanded or reshaped or broken. They were good people, unexceptional people. Perpetua's father was a quiet man, a German, from Odessa, given to long absences, days sometimes, out in the hills, from which he would return peaceful and oddly rested—younger-looking, as though the sandy blasts of wind across the land had polished him smooth, like a stone. He could read and write German fluently—an unusual ability, she learned later, for a man of his background and means. He took the German papers and read each one carefully all the way through, puzzling his forehead in the light from the coal stove as though solving some unpleasant mystery. And on Sunday mornings without fail, until the children were too old for him to do so, he would take each of them in turn on his knee—Magda and then Martin and then Perpetua—and he would tell them in German, *You are the light of my heart.* And then, while the children stood grinning expectantly, he would rise and wrap their mother's thickened waist in his big hands and whisper something in her ear—they never knew what, but they could tell by the look on her face it had to be the same thing each time. And she would smile and put the palm of her hand just so across his lips, as if she had placed a kiss there. She seemed to do this secretly, as she seemed to do all things, almost as though she worked some sort of magic in the everyday acts of living—in coaxing hot brown loaves of bread from the oven; or conjuring from that terrible gritty earth string beans fat and green as elves' stockings; or polishing the scuffed pine-board floor to a shine that made Martin giddy with sliding in his stocking feet, and Perpetua and Magda foolish with imagined dancing shoes and shimmering satin gowns the colour of birds' eggs. She was a large woman, broad-shouldered and wide through the hips, but she moved quickly and lightly, with the grace of love upon her limbs. No one outside the family would have called her beautiful. But there she was, nevertheless, soft and sudden and full-blown for them all like the wild roses by the gate in summer. And love, love, it was as if someone had dreamed them.

Only later, much later, did Perpetua realize her loving family had not taught love, but only collected it and stored it selfishly, like the bushel baskets of potatoes and mealy apples in the root cellar. No, they did not teach love. What they taught was this: everything for the family. And just the family. No friends to go visiting on a Saturday afternoon in December, no skating parties, no fall suppers; no group picnics at the river with baskets of other women's roast chicken and pickles and chokecherry strudels; no brandings, as they did not graze their cattle in the community pasture at the Sand Hills. Not even church, for they prayed at home, led by their father in German from the great black Bible brought from the old country. Always just the five of them. Yes, her parents were certainly to blame. When Perpetua thought this, she always paused uncomfortably over the word *blame*. But when she considered the effect of their love, it seemed that a little blame was necessary.

For many years, Perpetua had thought this failure to love was something wrong only in her. Then she had received a letter from Magda, poor Magda, alone in Saskatoon with a child, on the edge of her first divorce, who had written, *Tell me how it feels to go to bed each night and wake up each morning beside the man you love* (she had underlined *love*). *I feel sickened and empty. And my child, who is flesh and blood, asleep in the next room, her I can't even speak of, can't even look at some days without shame.* And Perpetua had read the letter twice over and wept terribly, big wrenching sobs, her apron up over her face and her shoulders shaking as though her body would break itself apart—wept, not for her husband, whom she did not love, nor for the children she had never had, whom she could not love either, but for poor Magda, whom she did love. She had wept that way until it was time for Joe's supper, and then, seeing him step heavily across the yard, she had slipped the letter into the breadbox, washed her face and greeted him, as she did each day, with a smile and a kiss.

And that letter had made everything clear. This is how it would always be. Magda, ending her marriage because she was waiting for love; Martin, never married, alone for years on their parents' farm; and Perpetua, married to a man she did not love. It was tragic. And terribly unfair. But, nevertheless, it was. Now, past seventy, with her parents and Magda long since buried in the little Catholic cemetery on the outskirts of town, and Martin rarely able to know her anymore, and only Joe to fill her days, it seemed a thing beyond worrying about, this love.

So when she looked out the window that Wednesday morning to see a woman in a yellow hat talking to Joe by his woodworking shop, she was taken aback by the great swelling that expanded her old ribs. The feeling came so suddenly and so powerfully that she stepped away from the back door and sank into a kitchen chair, her head swimming with the impossible emotion that trembled her fingers and sheathed her body in a fine layer of sweat. Her knees threatened to give way beneath her, not for Joe, but for the woman in the yellow hat. It took her a few moments to reassure herself that it was not Magda who stood awkwardly among Joe's larkspur, but Magda's daughter, Myra, who had written weeks ago that she might be passing through. Perpetua had not seen Myra since before Magda's divorce, not since Myra had gone off to live with her father in Manitoba. But that had been almost thirty years ago. The woman standing in the garden was not that rather homely, rather unhappy little girl she had known, but a woman approaching middle age, a woman who, for all Perpetua's rationalizing, *was* Magda, was Magda's blood, as she once said, Magda's body—with the same swelling thighs and narrow shoulders, the same straight yellow hair, the same uneasy stance, the stance of someone slightly cowed by the acceptance of her own graceless appearance. Perpetua had consumed all this detail in a flash as she'd looked briefly out the back door, seeing first Joe standing and nodding, clearly pleased with this visitor (so rare now), and then the woman in the yellow hat, wearing a white skirt and a striped blouse, holding a big straw shopping bag over one shoulder (did she mean to stay?).

Perpetua rose slowly and went back to the window, but both

Joe and the woman (she could not, no matter how she tried, think of her as Myra) had disappeared. Perpetua felt a small quiver of panic before she realized that Joe had no doubt invited her into his workshop. They were probably standing right now beneath all those neat rows of jars he'd glued by their lids to the low ceiling, to hold nails and screws and bolts; she was probably smelling wood shavings and pretending to admire (or genuinely admiring) his carvings: tiny cowboy boots and miniature horses, trains and racing cars and semi trucks (these latter mostly for children around town, and now their children). She would ask politely if he'd done the enormous, elaborately carved slab of varnished cedar out front that announced *Dunworkin*, and below that, in smaller letters, *Joseph and Perpetua Resch*. He could keep her there for hours, pointing out the intricacies of detail in a boot or a wheel or a horse's mane, the character of each different wood—the soft, cheap convenience of knotty pine or the hard, red richness of cherry (bloodwood, he called it), so rare and expensive out west—the grain, the weight, the variations in colour and texture, the shine that could be brought to any piece through sanding. How one could make even the softest wood gleam like marble. He could keep her there all night. But just as Perpetua was deciding whether or not to go out to them (she rarely left the house now, not much at all since the surgery), they both appeared at the doorway to the workshop. Joe pointed toward the kitchen, and the woman looked up, shading her eyes. Perpetua stepped back from the window, even though they probably could not see her. She knew what Joe had said as he pointed: "Your Auntie Pet's up at the house there. Go on up. She'll be real glad you're here."

So Perpetua busied herself around the kitchen, wiping the already spotless counters, moving canisters a fraction of an

inch into alignment, her hands shaking, and all the time thinking, Magda, Magda.

And then the doorbell.

"Come in," she called pleasantly, as if half-surprised.

When the woman opened the screen door and stepped into
the air-conditioned kitchen on a wave of hot, dry heat, with all
that sunlight still streaming in ribbons from her yellow hat,
Perpetua came slowly toward her, trying as much as possible to
hide the limp from the surgery, trying to swallow that terrible
lump in her throat. She took a breath and tried to smile, holding her hands out. "Well, well, look at this," she began to say,
but before she had finished, the woman turned away and covered her face with her big red hands. Magda's hands.

Perpetua took her in an awkward embrace. The woman held
the tips of her fingers pressed to her eyes. "What is it, dear?"
Perpetua asked (she could not say Myra). "Tell me. What's
wrong?"

The woman shook her head, still half-turned away, returned
Perpetua's embrace with one fumbling, fleshy arm that smelled
faintly of geraniums. The woman shook her head, lifted her
crumpled face as though in a tremendous effort to stop her tears.
She shook her head again and said something that Perpetua
could not hear, and in spite of the fact that she hated to do it,
Perpetua said, "What? What's that?" and the woman repeated
herself. Perpetua thought it was either "Glad to come back" or
"Sad to come back." Impossible to ask again.

The woman was embarrassed, Perpetua could see, so she
said, "Come in," and walked her slow, rolling walk to the table,
knowing it would give the woman a moment to pull herself
together before she followed. Perpetua sat down first, folding
her hands in her lap to still the trembling, then looked across
the table as the woman pulled out a chair for herself, planted

the heavy straw bag with great care at her feet and adjusted the waistband of her skirt. She removed her hat, lifting it too daintily for her hands, with two fingers at each side of the brim, and finally raised her face, gave that same crumpled smile. And it was Magda's face, streaky red and swollen from the tears and the heat—Magda, who had never been beautiful but who could look at you with a kind of light in her eyes that would set your very bones gently humming. Perpetua stared at the woman, so hungry for that feeling, just one small glimmer, that she almost reached across the table and grasped her by the shoulders to bring her closer. Perpetua looked, and she saw no light there. And then the woman was not Magda, but only Myra, with the red and swollen and lightless eyes. Perpetua felt her heart spill over again, not for Magda now, but finally, after all this time, for Myra. This woman. How could it be?

"So," Myra was saying, her voice soft and trembling, "it's been a long time."

Perpetua could barely catch the words. These last years, her hearing had been growing gradually worse, was so bad now that all conversation had a strange, dreamy quality. She leaned forward a little, working her hands in her lap, forcing the awful clenching of her heart to subside.

"How are you?" Myra asked. "What's going on with you these days?"

And before Perpetua could stop herself, she said, surprised at the sudden feebleness of her voice, "Nothing good. Joe had a heart attack last summer"—she thought Myra said, "I'm sorry, I didn't know"—"and I had surgery on my leg, and they put a pin in that's giving me a lot of trouble, it's painful, I don't sleep much anymore." And then she thought, Why did I say that? I didn't mean to say that. How terrible I must sound to her.

Myra said, "I'm sorry," again, and then, "Uncle Joe looks good. How is he?"

"What?" Perpetua said. "Joe?"

Myra raised her voice a little, leaned forward also. "Yes, how is he? He looks good."

"Yes." Perpetua nodded. "He's good. He's the same."

"He keeps busy out there, I guess."

"Yes," Perpetua said, "he keeps busy."

She thought of Joe in his workshop, every day now since he'd retired, puttering around, sawing and sanding and patiently scraping. He wouldn't admit it, but his eyes were going. He wasn't as good anymore with the fine detail.

"He didn't know me," Myra said, pushing out a little laugh. "I guess he wouldn't. He thought I was selling something."

Perpetua smiled and nodded. "Yes, they come around sometimes. Always selling something." She shrugged. "We never buy. Just from the Hutterites."

The woman nodded, leaned her elbows on the table, took them off again. "And how," she said, "how is Joe's family? He has a sister, doesn't he?"

"Yes," Perpetua said, thinking how strange it was that Myra should remember that. "In Medicine Hat. We don't see her much now. She's busy. With the grandchildren."

"Oh," Myra said, "she has grandchildren?"

"What?"

"She has grandchildren?"

"Yes. Great-grandchildren now. Two of them. Joe has pictures up," she said, rising slowly and leading Myra into the living room. Her hands had stopped trembling, but she was so conscious of the nearness of Myra's breath and her arms behind her that she still felt a little flutter of her heart. She wanted to touch her again, but it would seem strange. Myra would wonder. So instead, she pointed to where the pictures stood on a little shelf, all of them, in their brassy frames.

"There's more," she said, "out in the shop, all their school pictures. Joe probably showed you. Don't ask me their names. There's too many now."

Myra looked at the pictures, each in turn, making polite comments Perpetua did not always hear. She wished Myra would remember to speak up. She didn't like to keep asking her to repeat. Myra paused over a big black and white one in a wooden frame.

"That one," Perpetua said, "is me. And Joe. Our wedding picture." Stupid. Of course it was their wedding, Myra could see that.

Myra picked it up. "You were lovely."

"Oh," Perpetua said, shrugging. She knew she was not.

Myra placed the photograph gently on its doily, then picked up a small blurry snapshot of Magda and Martin sitting on one of their father's horses—Shotgun, Perpetua thought, though she couldn't really remember.

"This is Mother, isn't it," Myra said, pausing.

Perpetua wondered if she saw herself in that face. Surely she must, she must have pictures of her own. Wouldn't she?

"And Uncle Martin," Myra said. "How is he?"

Perpetua was about to say, Not good, but instead she said, "The same," and wiped a bit of dust away from the frame with her thumb.

"I'd like to see him," Myra said. "Is he still on the farm?"

Perpetua looked up in surprise. "No," she said, "he's in the home. For years now."

"Oh," Myra said, and put the picture down on the shelf.

She is ashamed, Perpetua thought, she thinks she should know these things. How could she know? She had been lost to them all for years, to Magda even. To Magda most of all.

"Your father," Perpetua asked then, because she felt she should, "how is he?"

"Fine. In Brandon still. With Lois. They're fine."

The stepmother, Perpetua remembered. The one who'd sent Magda Christmas cards faithfully, each year, with a brief letter and a picture of Myra standing posed in front of their upright piano, always the same pose, to show how much she'd grown. Lois, a stranger, who knew more about Magda's daughter than Magda herself did. It was too sad. Perpetua would not let herself think about it any longer.

"Where do you live now? Brandon?"

"Nipawin."

"Where?"

Myra raised her voice. "Nipawin. I teach there. Two and three."

Perpetua nodded. She watched Myra pick up pictures, set them back down, the same ones she'd already looked at.

"What, are you on a holiday?"

"Yes. Sort of. It's summer vacation." She smiled a little. "I guess that's my holiday."

"Out here?"

Myra turned away.

Perpetua straightened a couple of the frames. "You picked the worst time, July. You have air conditioning in your car?"

"Yes," Myra said without turning back. "It's hot, all right."

"I was never one for the heat," Perpetua said. "Everyone complains about winter. Not me. Joe neither. Nothing bothers him."

Then, finally, she asked, "Are you married?"

"Yes," Myra said, replacing the photograph she was looking at. "Robert Russell. We met at the university. His family is from around Kindersley. The Malcolm Russells. His grandparents are Aida and Clemens Russell . . . ?"

She trailed off.

Perpetua frowned. "Where is he? Working?"

"Yes," she said, "he had to work."

"You have children?"

"No."

Perpetua gave Myra's wrist a little squeeze and, though she was reluctant to let go, went slowly to sit in the armchair by the window. She made a motion for Myra to take a seat on the chesterfield.

"You want coffee?" she asked.

"No. Thank you."

"Juice? Water?"

"No, I'm good, thanks."

Perpetua folded her hands in her lap. The clock ticked out from the mantel, softly. Beyond the yellowed blinds, a car rolled past on the gravel road. She tried not to stare at Myra, though she felt as if she could swallow her whole with her eyes. That face. When she thought of it, her throat ached, and so she thought instead about Joe, working steadily out in the shop, listened for the sound of his radio or the high whine of the saw. But all was quiet.

"I guess," Myra said finally, fiddling with the hem of her white skirt, her eyes glistening in the yellow light, "I guess you and mother were pretty close."

Oh, Perpetua thought, oh, my dear child. And she wanted more than anything to pull that sad body to her, hold her close against her chest. Poor unlovely child. Child of my heart. My sister's child. Perpetua hid her hands beneath her apron.

"Yes," she said slowly, "there was just the three of us. We had no close neighbours. Just us."

Myra nodded. She wiped the tip of her awkward nose, stared up at a basket of silk flowers, then a brass cat, then a framed sampler Perpetua had been given years ago, decades, as a gift: *Act and suffer in silence.* She couldn't remember now who had given it to her, only that she had hated it always. She watched as Myra looked about the room. Finally, she could stand it no longer.

"You want to know about your mother?" she asked. "What do you want to know?"

Myra stared back at her.

"She was a good singer," Perpetua began. "She liked all animals. On the farm, she liked to be with the animals. Except mice, which she was afraid of. I don't know why; she wasn't afraid of anything else. She liked the horses, her and Martin both. I was always too scared. She liked the garden. She worked hard. We all did. She wasn't much of a one for housework." She smiled. "She got in trouble with Mum all the time for not doing this right, not doing that right. She baked an apple pie once, Mum left all the directions, but Magda used salt instead of sugar. Martin tried to feed it to the dogs so Mum wouldn't find out, but they wouldn't eat it. She got in trouble for that. She liked to sing." She lifted her hands. "I don't know. My memory is getting worse. If you ask questions, maybe I'll remember."

But Perpetua felt like a fraud, looking across at that unhappy face. This was not what Myra wanted to know. Not really. She leaned forward over her knees, as close as she could get without rising, and said slowly, clearly, "She was my sister. And I loved her. Just as I loved Martin. And my mother and my father. It was all we had. Do you understand? We didn't know anything but each other." She stopped here, hoping Myra *would* understand. "Our family, it was everything. More than that, I can't tell you."

Myra stared at the carpet, unblinking.

Perpetua rose and seated herself on the chesterfield next to her. She put one arm around her shoulders and thought, This is what we've all come to, then, all that love. How could she explain it?

"The truth is . . ." she began.

She looked up then to see Joe standing in the doorway, holding a small carved horse, a red one, gleaming with all the light of new marble. She could tell by the way he turned the figure slowly in his hands that he'd been standing there for some time. The horse, she knew, was for Myra. Though his carvings fetched quite a price in the city, he'd always given away far more than he'd sold. It was his way. He lifted the horse slightly, as if he would say something. But he did not. She stared back at him, with Myra between them, her face in her hands. They listened to the clock tick. And then, still looking at Joe, Perpetua said, "That's enough now." And she smoothed a hand across the back of Myra's hair. "That's enough."

Sand Hills

It wasn't that she lied. At least, I don't think she did—not what she would have considered lying, anyway. The thing about my mother was that she always loved a good story, right up until the day she died, tucked under my grandmother's wedding quilt on the chesterfield in the airless and darkened front room. She simply believed in a little embellishment, a little bending of the rules. She believed in constant and impromptu revision to keep things interesting.

It was a family trait that ended, apparently, with her. I would try sometimes, at her urging, to produce an adequately dramatized version of some dry bit of information I'd learned at school, something from history or science class, even bits of gossip I was privy to in the girls' washroom. I tried to recreate these stories the way my mother did, vividly, punching life and colour into everything; but I always ended up losing my place, confusing details, forgetting that I should have provided a vital fact sooner—*No, wait a minute, there were actually* two *Indians waiting around the bend, and one was really tired, or, no, he was sick, really*

really sick, and it was dark out, I should of said it was dark, and one of
the Indians, well, no, let me go back a bit.

This failure in me was a flaw my mother could never accept,
as if I had been born of alien and uncultivable flesh.

"That's all right, dear," she'd sigh, patting my leg halfway
through some dull and tortured tale, perhaps sensing my mis-
ery or simply no longer able to listen. Releasing us both from
my inadequacies. She would smile a little to keep me from feeling discouraged, scanning my face in a way that made me feel
she was still trying to decide whether or not we might come to
like one another.

Once she said abruptly, "I never told you enough," and I'd
thought at first she meant stories, that she was excusing me,
taking responsibility for my failure. But then she closed her
eyes and shook her head, patted my leg again, and said nothing
more. Her silence was my cue to read from one of the books
we were studying in school, *A Tale of Two Cities* or *The Old Man
and the Sea*. She liked best those set somewhere else, somewhere
other than the prairies, somewhere exotic, tropical, unleashing
the possibilities in a shell, a vine, a fish. She had me read *The
Pearl* twice during her illness and once more toward the end.
She was so small by then that I would tiptoe in quietly some
afternoons when the blinds were drawn and the winter light
was a dull, dusty gold, and think for a moment that she had
disappeared, simply evaporated from beneath the smooth blue
of the quilt, that it was her dust that floated all around me,
turned and glowed in the heavy light cracking from the edges
of windows where the blinds did not quite meet. Once I
thought, I could breathe her in now, her body like this, in such
fine particles. I could take all of her in. And I stood there
enchanted by the thought, both desperate and afraid to
breathe, caught in that one moment of pure, terrified longing.

"Mom?" she said then, and for a second I thought I'd spoken

out loud, felt my heart thudding against the back of my throat. But the quilt rustled and her still-dark head turned on the pillow.

"Oh, Del," she said, half-apologetic, half-disappointed, "I thought it was Grandma."

By the time my mother's illness transformed the front room into a sickroom, my grandmother had been dead nearly a decade, following fast on the heels of my grandfather. Everyone knew the two of them would go that way, so close together. After her funeral, people stood around at the fenced edge of the cemetery on the outskirts of town, smoking or dabbing at lipstick or simply leaning their bodies into the wind, agreeing on the inevitability of such near departures.

"A testament to their bond," the priest had said, the very words that seemed to be on everyone's mind. "A testament to God's will," he'd gone on to say at length, encouraged by the nods he'd received, "a testament to the glory of God and to the bond of man and wife, for each one of us, sinners all, each one of us, lambs and sinners all, which no thing, not even the cold hand of death, can put asunder."

Many thought he was going too far, though they agreed that his theory applied well to my grandparents.

"It's a fitting thing, Rose and Herb," they said, grinding the heels of their shoes in the patched grass.

"It's only right."

"We should all be so lucky."

The occasion of her death may, in fact, have been the only time my grandmother had been considered lucky. Rose Correy came from hard-on-their-luck people, the Sand Hill Mayhews (to distinguish them from the Town Mayhews, who owned the grocery store and were known to be fine, hard-working people despite the shocking markup on produce and perishables). Her father, Philip Mayhew, was seen as largely to blame for the family's misfortunes.

"Any fool can see that land over there isn't worth a rat's ass," they'd say around the coffee shop. "Can't grow nothing. Run some cattle, sure, but if you can't grow nothing . . ." And they would shake their heads and tip back their caps.

No one knew what made Philip Mayhew select for his homestead a wretched few acres on the edge of the Great Sand Hills—the worst possible tract of land in all Saskatchewan. We knew only that, on the long trip back to town after staking his claim, he'd stopped to drink from a slough, fell into a fever and died eight days later in a rooming house in Maple Creek, leaving his teenaged sons—dazed and stupid with grief—to break the land as best they could. Some said it was the lack of a father figure that made the Mayhews run wild, that their mother, left alone with five children on a farm where nothing grew but sagebrush, kocia weed and thistle, just gave up, let those kids do as they pleased.

"Drinkers and fighters," they said in town. "Four boys and no father—well, it's no wonder."

My grandmother, the youngest and the only girl, was tagged as guilty by association, though she herself had never been known to take a drink, not even a sip from the proffered bottles of her brothers' friends, and she was too small to be much of a fighter. I've seen pictures of her in my mother's album, a skinny child swathed in hand-me-down boys' sweaters or roughly made-over grown-up dresses (donated by town ladies to the *needy*, a word basically synonymous with Mayhew) that somehow gave her a disturbing air of unwholesomeness, the way the too-shiny fabric gleamed in the light and flapped low across the narrow bones of her chest. From the pictures, it's hard to tell what my grandfather saw in her, unless it was a certain waifishness, a vulnerability that appealed to his less noble instincts. In truth, the Correys weren't a far cry from the Mayhews, either in habit or spirit. The only difference was the family patriarch, Ted Correy, whose existence well into his nineties lent the illusion of family stability and discipline.

When Rose Mayhew married into the Correys, few would have claimed she was lucky, though some may have gone so far as to say she wasn't likely to do much better. But to the surprise of most, Herb and Rose seemed to fare well in married life. Rose grew plump and pinkish, could not, from the way she looked in those later years, possibly have been named anything but Rose. I've often wondered how her parents chose so accurately, why they had not selected the more popular Rosemary or Constance or even Violet. It has become a strange source of pride for me, the selection of that name, as though it spoke of a greater understanding and insight than the Mayhews were generally given credit for.

I suppose that the fibbing distinguished the Mayhews from the Correys as well. My grandmother, using what I came in later years to recognize as a considerable degree of creative licence, called it storytelling.

"We come from a long line of storytellers," she'd say to me sometimes when the Mayhew reputation around town (kept alive largely by the doings of her two youngest brothers, who still resided together on the family farm) came once more to my attention. "Mayhews always were fine storytellers," she'd say, pointing her little chin. "That's a thing to be proud of."

My grandfather, on the other hand, was known to remark that he'd never seen such a pack of BSers in all his born days.

"The whole bunch of 'em," he'd mutter, knifing into a pork chop, "talk you senseless. And what have they got to say for themselves? Not a goddamn thing."

My grandmother would murmur, "Herb," in that way she

had and then lift her eyebrows toward where I sat at the end of the table, pretending not to listen.

"What?" he'd bark. "It's the God's truth." Then he'd wink and say, "I got myself the best thing that ever come from them hills."

And my grandmother, I swear to this day, would duck her head and blush clear up to the roots of her hair, saying, "Herb," again, but not in the same way. And sometimes, seizing the moment, she'd add, "I wonder how Bob and Carl are doing." If my grandfather didn't respond, it was as good an answer as she could hope for. She'd sweep crumbs from the table into the palm of her hand and say, "About time we made a trip out there." Then smile over at me and add, "Make sure the old place hasn't blown away."

I'd been out to the Sand Hills frequently as a child, usually with my mother and my grandmother, sometimes with my grandfather in reluctant tow. When he did join us, he'd stay in the truck and smoke while my mother, grandmother and I went inside the unpainted farmhouse to visit with Great-Uncle Bob and Great-Uncle Carl. At first, I enjoyed those visits, sitting at the sagging kitchen table, sucking on a warm, dusty bottle of Dr. Pepper from the crate by the fridge, kept there solely for the purpose of mix. The two women cleaned and cooked, and the two men creaked back in their chairs, feet up against the edge of the table, drinking. And all four of them talked. It was dizzying, really, that chatter, and I found it intoxicating to sit there all but ignored, with my pop bottle wedged between knees drawn up to my chest, just listening.

"People can laugh all they want, but I'm telling you I seen it with my own eyes, that light, it was ghostly blue and it came each night and skittered over the same spot on the floor, till one night we pried up the boards with a shovel and there it was, a tin box stuffed to bursting with dollar bills, two hundred and twenty-seven of them, to be exact. Old Man Dubyk had come back for his money, sure as I'm sitting here today."

"What, Dubyk? Never had a penny to his name."

"Well, now you know why. Ha ha."

"That was the summer Forsby tried to swim his horse across the river."

"You were all down there drinking after Tom Fidder's branding."

"No, that was later, years later. You're losing your memory."

"It was a dare, wasn't it?"

"Emil Schlacht dared him."

"No, it was a bet."

"No, it wasn't, it was just Forsby. He was on his horse and halfway across before anybody realized."

"Well, it was in the spring. I know that because there was ice yet on the river and Mazey Cross was still alive."

"Mazey Cross! There's a name I haven't heard in years."

"That's where we carried the body, through the moonlight, I remember it was a full moon or near about, and she opened the door, all white-haired and holding up that candle just like an angel, you remember? And the light fell on poor Forsby and she looked at us all and then led us inside, where we laid poor Forsby on the kitchen table and all of us dripping wet and shivering like anything, and Foxy Eavell, who'd got to him first, crying and shaking like he might bust apart and Forsby so still it didn't seem possible. And then she covered him over with her good tablecloth and we knew it was done, and Mazey said so softly, 'You're through now, boys. Go on home. I think you're about through.'"

"Poor old Forsby."

"Poor old Mazey Cross. It was her heart got her in the end."

I sat quietly and listened and hoped my grandfather had dozed off in the truck outside, as he sometimes did. We all knew that when he leaned on the horn, it was time to go.

As I got older, I began to suspect my presence in the kitchen wasn't forgotten but rather indulged, that I was undergoing some rite of passage. Bob began to glance at me frequently, gauging my reaction to different stories. Did I laugh, was I embarrassed? Did I understand? Carl, on the other hand, continued to ignore me until one day late in the summer before my tenth birthday, when he turned to me abruptly and asked, loudly enough to make me start, "And what have you got to say for yourself?"

I froze, hands pressed to my kneecaps, toes curled over the edge of the chair.

"Well," Carl prompted, louder, "what can you tell me, Delly Mayhew?" He said it with an odd and inexplicable sneer, drawing it out in an ugly way—*Maaay-hew.*

Until that precise moment, it hadn't occurred to me that I was one of them, a Mayhew. My last name was Correy, of course, the same as my mother's, my grandmother's. But they were Mayhews, too. I was amazed that I had never included myself in their number, not consciously.

My grandmother and Bob had stopped mid-conversation, and my mother turned from where she stood at the kitchen sink, scouring a frying pan. Her long, dark red hair had pulled loose in the heat and hung down over her face, but I thought I saw alarm there, as if she was about to say something, then stopped, unsure herself what it might be.

I sat there dumb, looking from one face to another, sweat springing up all over my body, terrified by the weight of that moment, the expectation. Carl's sneer still hanging in the air over all of us. *Maaay-hew.*

The long blast of the truck horn startled everyone, even Carl. I sprang instantly to my feet, forgetting the sweaty pop bottle wedged between my knees. It hit the edge of the table and bounced to the floor, spinning absurdly on the cracked linoleum like in a party game. I stood there stupidly while the sticky pop foamed out around my feet.

My mother was the first to move, coming toward me with the dishcloth in hand.

"She's a Correy," Bob said, excusing me, swishing a mouthful of rye down his throat.

Carl looked at me narrowly, then at my mother, on her knees, mopping at the linoleum. "No," he said flatly, "she ain't."

It's strange how you don't see the most obvious things until someone points them out, like a deer at the edge of the highway at dusk, or those puzzles in children's books: *How many rabbits can you spot in this picture?* Then you wonder how you could have missed them. The fact that I was descended from the Mayhews was, of course, no surprise. But the real connection, the blood and flesh and bone connection, had not occurred to me until that day at the farm. In much the same way, it did not occur to me until the following autumn to wonder about my father.

Until that time, I'd been living under the assumption that I simply didn't have one. Oddly enough, I don't remember ever thinking about him much before then. Perhaps on some level I wished to believe that, like Thumbelina, I had been found by my mother in the petals of a tulip. Or perhaps my grandfather's presence more than adequately filled an obvious void. At school, for instance, I simply made the felt card or clay ashtray or whatever happened to be that year's Father's Day art project with my grandfather in mind. And each item was duly brought home and duly received without a sign of awkwardness on the part of any member of the family.

To the considerable shock of my grandmother, therefore, on a day not long after the unfortunate afternoon at Bob and Carl's, I turned to her in the car as we drove down Main Street, with all those poplar leaves scattering across the road like sunlight, and said, without preamble, "What happened to my father?"

As ever, she appeared unruffled. She simply pulled the big old Impala to a stop in front of the post office, retrieved her purse from the floor by her feet, where she always kept it when driving, and said pleasantly, "He ran away." Then she opened the car door and said, "Coming?"

I sat there, watching my grandmother swing neatly through the post office door, and pictured, instead, my father, inexplicably in top hat and tails, trudging away across the Sand Hills. Naturally, as he was running away, I pictured him from behind, but I've always thought it spoke largely of my creative inadequacies, that, in this only vision I ever had of him, I did not give my father a face.

When Bob married a widow woman from over near Swift Current, much to the surprise of everyone, he left the farm and Carl for the first time in his life. Everyone wondered what Carl would do without him. What Carl did, after about six months of solitary hard drinking, was load up a flatbed of rye bottles, some still half-full, and drive them out to the nuisance grounds. Then he stopped at the store, purchased five crates of Dr. Pepper, a paper sack of jawbreakers and all the cartons of Number 7s they had in stock, and headed back to the farm, stone cold sober possibly for the first time in more than forty years.

I had just turned seventeen, both my grandparents had been dead a few years, though not long enough for the crabgrass and sand flowers in the cemetery to completely cover their graves, and my mother was still simply feeling poorly, as she said; the cancer in her throat had not yet developed into the baseball-sized lump she would eventually keep hidden beneath the prettily scalloped edge of my grandmother's quilt.

Carl called one Saturday morning to say he'd been out in the Sand Hills after a yearling—the same damn one as last week, if we could believe that, she must have some jackrabbit in her, or antelope more likely, something wild anyway, that was for sure—and saw the chokecherries were ripe for picking and hanging as thick and heavy as grapes on the vine.

"I wouldn't mind putting some jam up this year," my mother said afterwards.

"Jam?" Just that morning I'd seen her sit down wearily on the back steps for ten minutes after taking only a few towels from the clothesline. I was catching her in these moments of exhaustion more frequently, and they were making me feel anxious and irritable. "You must be kidding."

She lifted the long red coil of hair from over her shoulder, then twisted it into a neat bun at the nape of her neck, the way she always wore it in hot weather—a motion that reminded me how young she still was. "We haven't had a good year for chokecherries like this since you were a little girl." She smiled and I turned away. "I remember because it was the same year Uncle Bob killed that rattler in the stable. Ten feet long if it was a foot. He kept the skin. It was the same year . . ."

She trailed off, as she had begun to do lately, looked instead down at her hands spread out on the kitchen table, fingers splayed.

I was seated across from her, folding a washload of socks and underwear, not much now, just hers and mine. I stopped, staring at her across the table, at her thin wrists, so white they were almost blue, and for a moment, I thought I hated her, hated them all and their stupid lies. Why couldn't they ever just tell the truth? And before I could stop myself, I said, "Where is it?"

"What?" she said, looking surprised.

I held a pair of socks balled up in my lap. "The ten-foot skin. Where is it?"

A funny kind of half-smile skittered across my mother's lips.

"I've never seen it," I went on, hating myself. "You'd think I would have seen it. All these years."

We stared at each other that way across the table, shame already worming its awful way up from my belly. Finally she said quietly, "Maybe you have. Maybe you don't remember."

"I'd remember," I said, though thinking now that maybe, in fact, I had seen it.

It was a trick all the Mayhews could do well: convince you that you'd seen things, done things, you never had. It reminded me of that card trick where the magician makes you think you've selected a card, though he has really just slipped it ever so gently into your palm.

"You'd have to ask Uncle Carl," she said. "I wouldn't know what happened to it."

She had me. She knew I'd never ask Carl. Though he had become a different man since he'd stopped drinking, I still harboured a certain distrust of him bordering on fear.

"Anyway," she said, "I think I'll go. I sure would like to see Uncle Carl." She turned away, took two plates from the cupboard, two forks and knives, two glasses, and began to set the table. "Who knows how much longer he's got."

After dinner, we loaded the car with empty ice cream buckets, filled a jug with ice water and headed north toward the Sand Hills. My mother was quiet, and I looked over more than once to see if she'd fallen asleep, her head rocking on that thin neck as if every bump in the narrow road would snap it. I was hot and tired and filled with a terrible shame that lapsed every few moments into anger. Of course, it wasn't anger at all I was feeling then, in those days before and during her sickness, it was simply fear.

"Should've gone this morning," I said irritably. "It'll be hot."

Her head bumped against the side window as the car lurched from the grid road onto the prairie trail that led out through the hills. "Sorry," I said.

I flicked the radio on, fiddled briefly with the one station we sometimes picked up out of Medicine Hat, flicked it off again. We both rolled the windows down, now that we were driving more slowly, listened to the pitched *whirr* of grasshoppers in the brush and across the sandy trail. It was high summer by then, and the wild roses had dried into their bright pink hips like crabapples, and the hot stench of sagebrush and ground cedar and the reeking hides of cattle baked in the sun blasted across the hills, seemed to shimmer in the very air with its awful weight. The sun off the hood of the car was like a blade. I watched as my mother shaded her eyes with one hand, then turned in her seat and looked backward out the rear window, watching the southern edge of hills slide past us.

"You know," she said after a while, "those hills are moving all the time. Every day. I never knew that. To think I've lived here my whole life and didn't know something like that. Did you know they were moving?"

I did. We'd studied erosion in science the year before, had taken a class trip to the Sand Hills to see it first-hand, but no one had listened to much the teacher said, unimpressed by something at once so familiar and so disdained. "Not all of them, though. Less than one per cent."

"Who told you that?"

"Mr. Starkey."

"Hmm," she said shortly. "He's not from around here, is he."

I knew she didn't expect an answer.

"Lloyd Stolley was saying the other day that in a hundred years they could be to Maple Creek," she said.

"What," I scoffed, "the Sand Hills?" I shook my head in scorn. My mother caught my look. "Probably not all the way to Maple Creek," I added, part apologetic. "They don't move that fast."

"Lloyd'd know," she said definitely, facing forward again. "He's got a nephew in engineering in Saskatoon. Or a cousin." She frowned. "Anyway," she went on, as if we'd been talking about this all along, "this is where Uncle Carl had his accident, somewhere around where this break in the hills falls."

This was news to me. "What accident?"

"His pelvis was crushed," she said with an air of surprise, as though I should have known.

"How did that happen?"

She sighed. "There was a party." In stories involving Uncle Carl, there was often a party. "He was standing between two cars parked along the side of the road. One of the Rawling boys pulled up behind. He was drinking, of course, and ran into the rear car. Not hard, just enough to pin him."

That explained Carl's limp, but something still puzzled me about the story. "The Rawling boys?" I said. "But they're young, aren't they? They're younger than you. What was Carl doing at a party with them?"

My mother smiled briefly. "Looking for me."

I wanted to ask more, but I felt baited and uncertain—was this just another story? I looked out the side window, watched juniper and snowberry blur smoothly together for a moment, then jolt as I hit another gully in the road. My mother sighed, shifted on the seat. My arms felt heavy and sluggish, as if I carried weights on my wrists, as if the blood was not quite reaching my fingers. I took an arm off the wheel and shook it.

"What's wrong?" my mother said.

"Nothing."

"Tired?"

A gopher skidded across the road and I winced at the small, soft *thump* it made under the tire.

"No." I felt her eyes on me and I turned toward the side window again. "No," I said, a bit sharply, "I'm not anything."

She sighed again and looked past me, up ahead a few yards.

"There's the boots," she said. She said it every time we passed them. I took my foot from the gas and let the car roll itself slowly by, knowing she wanted to look. "There," she said, "those three are mine." She pointed to two small cowboy boots and a rubber boot, all worn to shreds, turned upside down and jammed on top of the fence posts. But I already knew each one that had belonged to a Mayhew.

"Most are the boys'," she said, meaning my grandmother's brothers. "I guess they wore out the most boots."

I studied the long line of boots turned absurdly upside down. There was something disturbing about the way they stuck up into the air, all those heels pointing skyward.

"Those aren't all Mayhew," I said, knowing I'd said it before, possibly more than once.

"No," she said, "there's others."

"Who?" I asked, though I already knew.

"Oh," she said, "other hill families. Fidders have some, I guess, and Wallers. I don't really know. Everybody."

"I don't have any," I said after a moment.

"No," she said, watching the last few posts slide past us, "you don't."

I didn't know what I was waiting for her to say that day. I knew I was fishing, but I couldn't say why or for what. Maybe for one of her stories—not a lie-story, just a story. Already I missed the sound of her voice, the lulling rhythm of her words. *Those boots have been there as long as you and as long as me and as long as your grandmother, as long as people have lived and died on this land, and the first boot belonged to a boy, a small yellow-haired boy who was the first child born out here in these hills one autumn, just around harvest time, on a still evening when the moon rose fat and red from the dust of the men threshing hot, endless rows in the fields back of the hills. The first child, Henry was his name, and he was a beautiful child with yellow hair and the bluest eyes, blue like flowers you hear of in stories. Yes, he was the first child born here and the first child to die, poor Henry. To die in the winter here is a terrible thing . . .* Maybe that was the story I wanted, one of the first stories I remember her telling me, of yellow-haired Henry and that one terrible winter—or maybe something more. It wouldn't have mattered, though. By then, she had already begun to change the endings. Soon the stories would stop altogether.

Up ahead, we could see the farm wavering like a mirage in the afternoon heat, a trick of the atmosphere making it appear closer than it was. Making it appear larger than the great yellow dunes that surrounded it.

My mother's voice came so softly and unexpectedly, I started.

"Where *will* they be in a hundred years, then?"

I turned onto the long road that led into the farmyard.

"Delly," she said after a moment, as if I hadn't heard, "where will they be?"

Carl had already loaded buckets into the back of the half-ton and sat waiting on the steps drinking a Dr. Pepper when we pulled up to the house. He looked much smaller than the last time I'd seen him, as if all the flesh had simply dissolved on his bones. I glanced over at my mother to see if she'd noticed, too. But she was already hoisting herself out of the seat, and as I watched her, I thought, *Her, too. How thin they are, how terribly small.* I followed her up to the house where Carl was saying, "We picked ourselves a hot one." He cracked open another Dr. Pepper that had been waiting in the shade against the steps and handed it to me. I didn't want it but took it anyway. "Get you a coffee?" he said to my mother, who shook her head and looked up at the sun glaring against the house.

She shaded her eyes. "Should've brought some hats."

I looked over at her, puzzled.

"Plenty inside," Carl said, as if it had been rehearsed, "straw ones back of the kitchen door." Then he added, "Your mother's." As if we needed an explanation. As if we hadn't known all along the hats were there.

"I'll get them," I offered when no one moved, setting my bottle on the narrow step and squeezing past Carl, who leaned to allow me room.

"Back of the kitchen door," he said again.

We all knew they were there, of course. We'd used them plenty of times before. My grandmother had kept them specifically for the annual berry-picking. I grabbed two wide-brimmed ones off their hooks and then stopped, realizing I had never before been alone in that kitchen, and listened to the rhythmic ticking of the stove clock. The blinds were all drawn, curled and yellowing at the edges, and the linoleum had pulled up at the corners like tongues stiff with disuse, exposing the dirty wood beneath. Otherwise, the room looked much the same as I remembered it. The crate of pop still stood by the fridge and the table still swayed beneath stacks of newspaper, tobacco tins and stained coffee mugs. Over the back of the nearest chair hung what looked to be an old rag. I hooked it with my finger, held it up. It was an undershirt, worn and washed and worn again to a yellowy-grey, so thin I could see the pink tips of my fingers through the fabric. The initials C.M. still showed faintly in blue ink on the tag. I quickly dropped it back on the chair and left the room, embarrassed at having held something at once so intimate and so sad.

"You ever heard of a fella name of John James?"

Carl and I were under the chokecherry trees, and my mother had gone back to the truck to rest in the shade. I slapped at a mosquito on my thigh.

"John James," he repeated. "Said he come from around here, but I never heard of no Jameses."

I squinted up at him briefly from where I knelt in the hot, soft sand, but he had his back to me, stretching his thin arms high up into the branches.

"Best ones always at the top," he said, bending a long branch toward me, pinning it beneath his arm. I noticed that he picked by closing his thumb and index finger over a bunch of berries and then pulling straight down so they fell into his palm. Both his hands were stained a bluish purple. I hooked my bucket over my wrist and continued plucking neatly, berry by berry.

"Anyway, this John James," he continued, "I thought maybe your mother might've said something about him one time."

I plunked two berries into my bucket, slapped at another mosquito. It left a smear of blood on my calf. "No," I said, licking my thumb and rubbing it away, wondering with distaste, as I always did, whose blood it was. "Never heard of him."

I glanced at Carl, but he was busy pulling and dropping and pulling again. It must have been hard on him, I thought, out on this farm all alone. Mayhews weren't meant to be loners.

"There were some thought he might have come from the Hutterites over in Estuary," he went on, "but I never did. He didn't have that Hutterite look."

I grimaced but said nothing.

"What I think is he wasn't from around here at all, though he told everybody in town he'd come from the hills and wasn't nobody questioned him. We all thought he meant Sand Hills, of course, but I guess he could have meant any hills at all."

I shifted my nearly full bucket to the other wrist, rubbed at the welt the wire handle had left on my flesh.

"Here." Carl handed me an empty bucket from the pile behind him. "He come to town, must've been about '66 or, no," he said, thinking, "it was '67 because we had the big centennial do that year. Anyway, this John James come to town, and do you know what he was selling?"

I shook my head in spite of myself.

"Bibles." Carl spat a little when he said it and a drop fell on my forearm. I forced myself not to wipe it off on my shorts, not right away, not while he was looking. "Not just any Bibles," Carl said, beaming at me as if about to deliver a punchline. "Bibles"—he paused for dramatic effect—"he wrote out by hand."

I looked at him skeptically and he nodded.

"Two of them," he said, shifting the branch to his other arm, "one finished and one still in the works." He chuckled. "I can see you don't believe it, and I didn't believe it neither. Till I saw one for myself."

"You saw one?"

"Yup." He nodded. "And if you still don't believe me, you got someone that'll back me up right there." He pointed his chin in the direction of the truck and my mother's head resting in the corner of the open window.

I stared at him. "She never mentioned anyone named John James."

He shrugged. "That's neither here nor there. But he come to town with them Bibles and made quite a laughingstock of himself. People made fun of him, called him names and such, on the quiet at first, but it wasn't too long before people started calling him The King to his face, short for King James. And worse. But your grandpa, he got kind of friendly with him, not to put that past a Correy, and took him under his wing, sort of."

"Why would Grandpa do that?" I asked doubtfully, for Grandpa was not the kind to take anyone, especially a stranger, under his wing.

"I can't speak for them that don't speak for themselves. All I know is he let him stay in the attic room for a few weeks." He shook his head. "I knew from the start he was trouble."

I'd stopped picking now, but Carl kept raking his fingers through the leaves, so mechanically I wanted to slap his hand.

"What kind of trouble?"

"Oh, the usual kind. He was heading east, he said, looking for work. And you know what that means."

I didn't but nodded anyway.

"Your grandpa put him up for a while, thinking sooner or later he'd figure out there wasn't nobody going to buy them Bibles. But John James thought he was on to something, I guess, because he just kept going door to door, peddling. Of course, it didn't take long before he'd gone to the same doors two, three, sometimes four or five times."

Carl let go of the branch, and I jumped back as it thwacked against the sky. He reached up, grunting, to pull down another, and I noticed the sweat stains under his armpits had an unhealthy-looking brownish tinge.

"Started to make a nuisance of himself, and one day a few of the men from town went over to your grandpa's and told John James to pack up his Bibles and head on out, keep right on going."

"Did he?"

"Oh yeah." Carl bent for a new bucket. "He left all right." He paused again, looking up at me to see if he could draw out the suspense any further.

"And?" I said impatiently. "That's it?"

"No, ma'am." Carl shook his head. "That is not it. He left town all right . . . but not before he nailed every one of them Bible pages to the church."

"The Catholic church?" I said.

"Yes, ma'am, the Catholic church. I was there the morning we found them and so was your mother, and we stood along with a bunch of others from town and stared at those pages, flapping away like a million wings, like that old church might suddenly go skyward." He looked up as he spoke, as if he might see it there among the clouds. "I'm surprised your mother never said nothing."

I waited for a minute to see if he would laugh, but he just took out a hanky, wiped sweat from his upper lip and said, "Are you going to keep picking or not?"

I looked back at the truck, at my mother's dark red head leaned up against the open window, at the fine, pale curve of her chin. It looked as if she'd shifted position, and I wondered whether she was really sleeping or just lying awake, listening to

Carl's story through the hot hum of grasshoppers. I knew without a shadow of a doubt that if I asked her later, she'd say she
never heard a thing.

I never did ask her later. Not later that day at the Sand Hills
nor on the long, silent drive home, nor in the following
months, when I spent most of my free time at her side, reading
stories or just sitting, pretending not to notice as she gradually
grew smaller and smaller under that quilt until finally she just
disappeared—though not in the way I imagined it that afternoon as I stood mesmerized by golden bits of light. Her death
was a darker thing, in the end. A sadder thing. There wasn't
much beauty in it after all.

And I never did ask her about John James. Instead, I harboured for many years the firm belief that Carl was trying to
tell me something that day under the chokecherry trees, that he
was trying, either with or without my mother's consent, to tell
me something about my father. And for many years, I believed
my father to be that mysterious John James, the drifter, the
zealot, the man from the hills of nowhere. I was wrong, of
course. John James wasn't my father. I heard the whole story,
years later, from an aunt I'd got friendly with, my grandfather's youngest sister. It wasn't very interesting. He was just a
farm boy from across the line in Alberta. They were both kids.
They made a mistake: Life went on. End of story.

* * *

I have an image of my mother in a lavender dress, her body
awkwardly canted against the white rails of a farmhouse porch,

shoulders erect, one foot arched neatly outward to lend the illusion of confidence. It is late afternoon and the spindled shadows of rails stretch away from her, casting slats over clumps of crabgrass sprouting slow and painfully from the dirt. She is young, younger than I am now. Her hair, long and a brighter red than I remember it, is held back in a tight, unflattering fashion by bobby pins at her temples. I can't say whether or not she is smiling, or what she is doing with her hands, whether they are propped graceless and freckled against the railing or fall lost and anonymous in the folds of her skirt. I don't know where the image comes from. Likely, it's one of my own fabrication—like that image of my father running away across the Sand Hills. And there are others, of my grandmother, my grandfather, even of myself. I have carried them around with me since childhood like malleable photographs I can add detail to over the years, if I choose, or do not choose, to expand the narrative. At least, that's how I've come to understand it. This image I have of my mother could be her lie or my own. I know only that behind the porch rails, behind the house, there is a red barn with the loft door hanging slightly off one hinge, flapping and creaking in even the slightest wind. There is a rusted-out half-ton behind it, and three granaries weathered to the same grey as the dirt, and just a few yards farther, sunk oddly almost below the level of the horizon, a sparse row of cottonwood and caragana someone once intended for a shelter belt. Beyond the trees, so far in the distance they can hardly be seen, the smooth, pale Sand Hills shoulder up from the prairie.

•   •   •

After my mother died, I saw it as a kind of duty to stop by the farm every so often, just to see how Carl was getting along, if he needed anything. Sometimes I cleaned a little, washed the dishes, swept the floor. Carl would sit at the kitchen table and watch me.

Almost always he said, "I guess it's just me and you now."

"There's Bob," I'd say each time. And he'd mutter, "Bob," and flick his hand dismissively. It became a sort of routine for us.

"You don't look much like your mother," he said one day. I kept sweeping, my back turned toward him.

"No," I said, bending to reach the dustpan, "I guess I don't."

"No," he said again, as if to reinforce it. And then, "You ever ask her about that John James I told you about?"

I tipped the dustpan into the garbage bag.

"No," I said, propping the broom in its place behind the fridge.

"Hmm," he said, a short, sharp sound. He leaned back in the chair, propped his feet awkwardly on the edge of the table, trying for the old easiness in his bones.

"You need a wash done?" I asked, tying the top of the garbage bag shut.

"That's funny you never asked her," he said. "Seems like maybe you would've."

I lugged the bag to the front door, set it outside. The sun was just beginning to dip below the bluing hills and the air had turned cold. I stood watching for a moment before I returned to the kitchen.

"I'll run this garbage to the burning barrel on my way out," I said, taking my coat from a hook by the door.

"I guess I never told you I read one of them Bibles." He nodded, his eyes shining in the fading light. I wondered whether he'd started drinking again. "That John James," he said, "he had nice handwriting. Must've took him a long time to write it because it sure took me a hell of a long time to read it." He tipped forward, the chair hitting the linoleum with a *thud* that seemed too loud for the moment. "I read it all," he said. "Ask me anything."

I sighed and pulled my coat on.

"Go on," he said, "anything."

"Okay," I said, trying to be funny, "how does it end?"

Carl frowned. "That's the thing," he said. "It's a good story, but it don't end well."

Just for a moment, I caught that image of my mother, not the one where she's standing against the porch rails in the sunlight, but the other one, her small body under the blue wedding quilt barely making a rise in the fabric, and all that yellow dust turning slowly in the air, as if I could touch it.

Carl leaned across the table.

"If it'd been me," he said, "I'd of told a different ending. But not John James." He gaped at me, wide-mouthed and toothless across the gathering darkness. "He stuck to that story word for word. Didn't change nothing."

Acknowledgements

I wish to offer thanks to the following:

Tim Birch, Steve Price, Greg Hollingshead, & Esi Edugyan; the Alberta Foundation for the Arts; UVic's creative writing department, & Jack Hodgins in particular; Anne McDermid; Phyllis Bruce & everyone at HarperCollins; Dennis & Rita Thorburn; John Baker; & most of all, my mother, Lorraine Bitz, generous always.

"Small Comfort" first appeared in *The Malahat Review*; "Lillie" appeared in *The Antigonish Review*; "Bloodwood" appeared in *Prairie Fire*. Thanks to the editors of those journals.

JACQUELINE BAKER was raised in Saskatchewan, studied creative writing at the University of Victoria, and is a recent MA graduate of the University of Alberta. Her work has appeared in magazines such as *Grain, Prism, The Antigonish Review* and *The Malahat Review.* She lives with her family in Edmonton, Alberta, where she is at work on her first novel.